render

a novel by

W. Joseph O'Connell

This book is presented as a work of fiction and is dedicated to the

Fallen Heroes of Desert Rogues

1-64 AR, 2ABCT

Gone But Never Forgotten

1

He was a rat, forced into a cage and finding himself with all the other rats, like walking through Chinatown and going home, noticing the odor had stayed in his clothes. New York's Chinatown was the first place in his life he had seen a dead person, covered in a white sheet soaked with blood. He was a kid when that happened, and he got a sick feeling in his stomach whenever he smelled Chinese food.

A group of white buses carrying several hundred soldiers began the journey in the middle of the afternoon. On a rural highway that cut through a swamp in the Georgia pines, it was the start of a long trip. Joe Cuero was one of more than a hundred Army soldiers on one of the buses. He tried to release his mind from thought as he watched a blur of green vegetation pass by the nearest window.

"Take a good look, boys," someone called out from the back of the bus. "You're not going to see anything that looks like this for a long time."

The hardest part of going on a combat deployment was leaving behind his wife and three sons. Joe was thirty-six when he joined the Army at the start of 2006. He deployed to Iraq for The Surge the following year. He was assigned to a tank company known as the "Wildbunch" of the 1ST Battalion, 64TH Armor Regiment, based at Fort Stewart, Georgia, the home of the dogface soldiers of the U.S. Army's 3rd Infantry Division.

Joe was born and raised in Texas. Home never seemed so far away. Through the window of the bus, he watched a group of bikers dressed in patriotic colors ride alongside the convoy as it traveled north on Interstate 95 toward Hunter Army Airfield in Savannah. The bikers joined a police escort for the half-hour trip to the airfield.

Soldiers boarded a plane that took them to Germany, where the plane was refueled before flying to Kuwait. The plane landed in Kuwait in the middle of the night. Soldiers were weary from travel as they climbed aboard buses that took them to Camp Buehring for two weeks of preparations until the final stage of their journey to Iraq. Night had fallen, and Joe sat quietly as the convoy made its way to Camp Buehring. The interior of the vehicle was shrouded in darkness, its windows covered by curtains drawn shut as a security precaution.

A laptop computer flickered to life in the darkness. A soldier held up the computer as it played a pornographic movie, to the amusement of those not yet asleep. Pornography was illegal in Kuwait, but the bus driver seemed unfazed by the display of ugly Americanism. On the video, a dark-haired woman wearing a red bra and panties exchanged vigorous oral sex with a man before engaging in melodramatic intercourse.

The soldier interrupted the entertainment by shutting off the computer. "Turn that back on, I'm not finished yet!" came a shout of protest from the back of the bus. The soldiers who packed the vehicle erupted in laughter.

It was past midnight when they arrived at the camp and gathered equipment from the buses and freight trucks that had joined the convoy. Camp Buehring was something like another planet to Joe. It functioned like an immense machine, even in the middle of the night. Rucksacks and duffel bags were consolidated and staged outside an enormous tent where, over the next few hours, soldiers attended orientation briefings before being released to get some precious sleep.

Some of his buddies said they were going to a phone center to call home, and he went with them. He phoned his wife, Viviane, but she did not pick up. An odd thought flashed in his head at that moment.

"Jesus Christ," it occurred to him, "She has a new boyfriend already." He laughed softly at the intrusion, then called his parents. They talked for about fifteen minutes. When everyone in the group had finished and stepped out of the phone center, it was four-thirty in the morning. The eastern sky was already turning pale blue as dawn approached.

Wakeup was at nine-fifteen. Joe stepped outside the sleeping tent and was blinded by the glare of the sun and a sweltering heat unlike anything he had ever felt. The desert landscape was dotted with tents, metal buildings, and tan-colored military vehicles of all shapes and sizes.

His platoon of sixteen tank crewman had been removed from its armor company and attached to an infantry company prior to leaving Georgia. Having a longstanding rivalry throughout modern Army history, tankers and infantrymen had joined forces on this combat tour, which was expected to last fifteen months. The platoon fell under Baja Company, bringing its four Abrams tanks and their crews prepped and ready for combat. Baja Company was a group of more than one hundred infantrymen organized into platoons of about thirty-six men each. Joe's tank platoon was augmented with a handful of infantry soldiers to beef up its strength, but it was still at half the manpower of a regular infantry platoon.

On the first day in Kuwait, the mongrel platoon of tankers and infantrymen walked twenty minutes in the mid-morning heat to the motor pool for a class on the Army's High-Mobility Multipurpose Wheeled Vehicle, the Humvee. The short walk was one of the most physically demanding events of Joe's life. It was only minutes before his heels started to blister. Searing heat had him gasping for air and sweating profusely.

Over the next few hours, soldiers checked the armored trucks, discussed safety features, and verified that tools and other items assigned to the vehicles were present. When it was time for lunch shortly after twelve o'clock, they trudged across the desert to the chow hall. They used dumpsters located along the route to discard water bottles that had gone dry long ago.

The first heat casualty occurred at lunch. An infantryman at the dining facility filled his tray with food, placed it on a table and passed out, tumbling backward onto the floor. His buddies rushed to his side, and within minutes he was slumped in a chair, conscious but groggy.

The soldiers were given the rest of the day to themselves. They were released from training to go about personal business. Joe accompanied a group that went to the camp store. He spent less than ten dollars on a reflective belt, which was a mandatory safety item for everyone walking around the camp at night, and a bottle of Gatorade.

He returned to the tent and laid down on a cot for a few hours of sleep. When he woke up, he went to dinner and called his wife. Hearing her voice lifted his spirit and sent him back to the tent with a bounce in his step. It was a long first day in Kuwait. Until Joe talked with his wife, the first day in Kuwait seemed like the start of a life sentence in prison.

2

The second day of preparation in Kuwait was a series of classroom sessions and briefings in a large, brown tent. The first lecture was about equipment designed to jam Improvised Explosive Devices the enemy was setting off remotely via radio frequencies. Afterward, a British Army officer gave a talk on preventing fratricide. Then another class on IEDs focused on how to spot them and what to do after that. The presentation included video clips of American soldiers being blown apart by roadside bombs.

Between classes, Joe sat on a concrete block outside the tent and lit a Newport cigarette. Seated next to him was Austin Briggs, a big Oklahoman with straw-colored hair who was on his third tour in Iraq. Briggs was a pragmatist, having made up his mind long ago that the most important factors in staying alive in combat were utilizing common sense and keeping his gear in top working condition. When it came to his equipment, his top priorities were the M4 carbine and Night Vision Devices (NVDs) the Army had issued to him. He was constantly cleaning and checking them.

Briggs joined the Army a few weeks after September 11, 2001, and by the invasion of Iraq in early 2003, had established himself as one of the best soldiers in his tank company. He saw his first combat that year with the Thunder Run into Baghdad and returned in 2005 for another tour. Briggs climbed the ranks to become a sergeant but was busted down for being disrespectful toward authority. He usually sported a few days of unshaved stubble on his squared jaw that resembled a block of granite. Officers and the senior enlisted soldiers didn't seem to mind Briggs being out of Army regulations with his scraggly face, in part because of his reputation as an old school tanker who kept his head in the heat of combat.

Briggs pulled a worn notepad from his breast pocket, studied it for a moment and said, "Hey Mexicano. You take notes from these experts on how to stay alive when we get to our sector?"

"Why don't you tell me?" Joe said. "This is your third go 'round over here."

"You can't show someone what it's like over here. You can tell them, but they won't get it until they see it in person," Briggs said. His demeanor was usually cynical toward anything that came from official channels. He walked around as if something you couldn't see weighed upon his massive shoulders, like a burden he could not shake. He looked down at the sand while Joe smoked. "I'm trying not to get into the dumps today. Yesterday was a pretty good day. I haven't gotten too far down into the dark places."

Briggs was the first soldier Joe met upon reporting for duty at Fort Stewart. Ten years younger than Joe, the seasoned warfighter hassled him nearly every day back at home station in Georgia. For more than a year, nothing Joe did as a tank crewman was good enough. Joe didn't like it, but he kept his mouth shut, learned his job and followed directions until Briggs finally stopped bothering him all the time. Briggs gave him shit for being a Hispanic from Texas but, seeing as how Briggs was six-and-a-half feet tall and two-hundred thirty-five pounds of Oklahoma white boy, Joe didn't pay him any mind about that.

"Can I get a menthol?" Briggs asked.

Joe reached into his pack and gave him a cigarette. Briggs took a drag and let the smoke curl out of mouth. "I was doing some homework for a college class last night, but my head wasn't there. I started thinking again. Just things in general. Things from the past. Everything got bottled up and I felt closed in again, so I figured I would take a break. Maybe that's what was messing me up, you know?"

Joe nodded, his head down as he stared at the sand. Briggs had a way of talking about what he called the dark places, a way that drew Joe in, trying to see if he could help Briggs figure things out.

Briggs stayed quiet for a few drags on the cigarette before he started again. "I took out some pictures and started looking at them. "There's one of me from when I was in JROTC in high school. It's one of me with a saber from when I was in the color guard at homecoming. I looked at it and I wanted to cry, because I looked at that picture and I was like, damn, the me in that picture never would have thought, ten years later, I would be going through what I'm going through up to this point. I thought, in that picture, ten years later I would have this, and I would have that. Life's going to be good."

Joe dropped the cigarette butt in the sand and ground it under his boot. "Is it bad?"

"I can't say it's good. But it's not bad, either, because it's a mixture of both. You have your good and you have bad. And I couldn't help but think, if I could just go back into that picture and knowing what I know now, I could prevent everything."

"Who doesn't feel that way?" Joe said.

"Maybe so, but I called an old friend of mine last night. I've known him since elementary and we were in boot camp together. We went to different high schools so we kind of split ways but stayed in touch. After boot camp he went to a different unit. I was at Stewart and he was in Italy, and every now and then he would check up on me. He got out of the Army after a few years, but after looking at that photo last night I went to the phone center and called him and immediately broke down. I don't know why. I just started venting, and it felt good. I guess I just needed to cry, just needed to let everything out. I haven't done that in a while. That's one of the reasons why I drink, to be honest. I get drunk to get myself sad on purpose and let it all out, to cry it out so I can get some sort of relief. And it felt weird to do that last night. It really made a big difference, like a lot of boxes got taken out of my storage room last night." Briggs let out a long sigh and dropped his head onto his chest.

"Good deal, man," Joe said. "Let's get back to work."

The platoon stayed outside the tent for another training session on operating the trucks. The speed limit on the camp was twelve miles per hour. Drivers kept the trucks at a crawl on the sandy trail, with soldiers taking turns behind the wheel in the mid-morning heat. The slow pace hampered the trucks' air-conditioning capabilities from providing much relief to the soldiers jammed inside. Under a cloudless sky, Kuwait was barren and broiling. There was nothing on the flat horizon but a heat mirage. They took a break for lunch and returned to the tent to continue sleeping off the jet lag. The tent resembled a trade show of laptop computers, with dozens of them being used for personal use and creating a low soundwave that ushered Joe to sleep.

The tanks were not in Kuwait. It was a significant problem. Each day, officers and senior enlisted soldiers were told from higher echelons it would be any day now. But there was maintenance to be done on the tanks, which were shipped from Georgia by oceanic freight. Potential ill effects of a journey by sea, especially those of extreme moisture and the salt in the air, had planted seeds of worry throughout the tank company. Time was needed to ensure the tanks and weapons systems would be combat effective for the mission in Iraq, and everyone was becoming restless.

The weather turned in a sudden and unexpected way. The hellish heat of the previous days dropped to ninety-five degrees when a sandstorm cooled the air and dimmed the sky with a bronze haze.

As the environment changed, so did the training. Tankers and infantrymen each delved into their separate, doctrinal natures. Fine tuning for combat had begun in earnest. Infantry soldiers rendezvoused with their Bradley Fighting Vehicles and started training in the Kuwaiti desert. At least someone had found their horses, Joe thought. Confined to the tent while awaiting the arrival of the tanks, he went about the daily routine of cleaning his M16 rifle and M9 pistol. The weapons were oiled and functioned smoothly as Joe repeatedly conducted checks to ensure they would work properly when needed.

In the days that followed, the slow, methodical start shifted to an intense training cycle that pushed everyone to the limit. The temperature skyrocketed to one-hundred and twelve degrees. Joe's hands and feet became horribly blistered, and a stiffness dug into his legs no matter how much water he drank. The tanks finally arrived, and maintenance got underway.

The tankers mounted their vehicles and left the camp for two consecutive days to test-fire every weapon system in the arsenal, from the 120mm cannon of the Abrams tank to the 9mm Beretta pistol assigned to each crew member. A tank crew normally consisted of four personnel, but Joe was part of a three-man crew, and his team worked diligently to dial in the weapons and scored nearly perfect results with the tank's main gun at a range of just over one thousand meters.

Near the end of the two weeks of preparation in Kuwait, the tankers reported to an array of metal containers arranged in a manner to resemble an enemy compound. The platoon was organized into two squads of nine men each to clear the objective, an infantry technique somewhat foreign to most of the tank crewmen. The tanker's motto: "Death before Dismount," had no bearing as they prepared for The Surge into Baghdad. They committed a variety of mistakes while struggling through the training exercise, which was monitored on video by civilian evaluators. An after-action critique revealed they moved too slowly and set security on rooms already cleared, which degraded their combat effectiveness. Some positive aspects noted in a later review were that they maintained effective communication within the teams and adapted well to the scenarios that were presented.

The training in Kuwait came to an end, and under nightfall the platoon staged its tanks to be loaded onto heavy trucks for the trek to Iraq. Final hours of free time were dedicated to calling home and emailing loved ones, washing laundry, and playing billiards at the camp's recreation center.

On the last day in the safety of Kuwait, Joe called his wife, checked email, and slept. The temperature reached one-hundred and fifteen degrees. Just before dinner, the first sergeant of Baja Company gathered the infantry soldiers and tankers together. More than a hundred combat soldiers were assembled around First Sergeant Jerry Payton for a talk that lasted over an hour, and Joe's attention was upon every word spoken by the senior enlisted man of the company.

Payton was an infantry legend. Not much was known among his men about where he was from, or how many times he had been shot at, blown up, or left for dead by the enemy in his more than twenty-five years in the Army. His immense frame was crooked from too many surgeries to count, but his perpetually squinted eyes and baritone voice commanded respect. It was the eve of a low-level flight across Iraq, aboard a C-130 aircraft that would take Baja Company to its destiny across terrain held by enemy forces.

"When you get on that bird tomorrow, have your fucking game faces on!" the first sergeant barked. "There are insurgents who want to fucking kill you, cut your head off and embarrass our country. I want us to fight as a company and survive as a company.

We are looking fucking outstanding. Nobody brings firepower to the battlefield like this fucking company right here."

The first sergeant briefed the company on its sector of responsibility. It was a place called Amiriya, a small but densely populated neighborhood in southwestern Baghdad. Baja Company would hit the ground hard to send a message to the most prevalent cell operating in sector, al-Qaeda in Iraq. They would relieve an Army unit that had not made its presence felt in its area of operations.

"Very seldom have they seen Bradleys running around in our sector," said the first sergeant. "If you feel threatened while on a mission, eliminate that fucker. Be professional, be polite, but be prepared to fuck them up."

The first sergeant went over the defense plan for operations at the rearward position, Camp Liberty, one of the largest Forward Operating Bases in Iraq. The plan required soldiers to know the locations of bunkers, aid stations, and casualty-collection points, in the event the base received mortar fire or was overrun. He emphasized the importance of maintaining accountability of sensitive items such as weapons, communications equipment, and optics. The briefing ventured into keeping weapons in good working order, maintaining situational awareness, and performing checks and inspections prior to starting every mission.

Many of the attacks on friendly units were being attributed in part to the complacency of the troops on the ground. Every soldier in the company was to remain focused, vigilant, and avoid setting patterns. "If we leave the FOB and go into our sector, we can't take the same route every fucking day. We're just asking to get fucked up," Payton said. Despite the harsh tone of his speech, the first sergeant finished on a more lighthearted note.

"I want you to have fun while you're here," he said. "You're going to see some crazy-ass shit. My last time here, we got video of some Haji fucking a donkey. Some of you are going to get into fights while you're here and beat each other up. I think it's funny. I will never get pissed off about you fighting if that's how you relieve stress."

With that, the first sergeant turned the meeting over to the senior medic of the battalion, Staff Sergeant Eric Gratton. A veteran of Desert Storm who had the respect of every soldier in the unit, Gratton was a quiet professional, and an expert in the craft of keeping soldiers alive in combat. He was a stocky, grey-haired man with a solid jaw. His gruff appearance was belied by his care for soldiers and soft-spoken manner.

"I've seen enough, and I don't want to see anymore," Gratton said. "For those who are here for the first time, I'll just say this, take care of each other."

3

The infantry company headed north to Iraq while the tank platoon stayed in Kuwait. There was not enough room on the transport plane. To make matters worse, a heavy sandstorm blew into the desert camp. With nothing on the training schedule, time was idled away on the internet. At the recreation center, Joe found his fellow tankers playing billiards and table tennis. He slumped into a leather recliner and started watching television.

"Get your ass up."

It was Staff Sergeant Deuce Badger. He was Joe's section sergeant, a man with a vile disposition toward the lower enlisted soldiers. Among his peers, he kept to himself.

"Is your tank squared away? Why are you sitting here?" Badger asked.

"Staff Sergeant, all the work got done. The tanks are packed up and being sent forward," Joe said. He was puzzled, knowing the staff sergeant was aware of this fact. As usual, the noncommissioned officer was playing a trick, up to his old games.

"So, now you got an attitude, Cuero?"

"No, staff sergeant, I don't have an attitude. It's my fault. Do you have something for me to do?"

"Yeah. Go find Fisher and that fuck up, Briggs, and clean the tent. It's a cluster fuck in there."

“Roger that, staff sergeant.” Joe walked alone back to the tent. The departure of the infantrymen left it quiet and dark. Fisher was there, and he cursed Badger when he heard of the section sergeant’s orders, but he helped sweep the tent and take out the trash. When they were finished, Joe laid down to sleep without dreams for the first time in days.

They flew the following day. A Boeing C-17 transport plane landed without incident at Baghdad International Airport in the middle of the night. Within minutes, a convoy of buses brought the tankers to Camp Liberty. They sifted through piles of duffel bags and rucksacks for their gear as attack helicopters circled nearby, chased by enemy tracer fire amid the darkness. The tank platoon’s tent sat behind a row of concrete walls. Joe settled onto the top rack of a bunk bed. He glanced at his watch before falling to sleep. It was just past four o’clock in the morning on his first day in Iraq.

He got up at eleven-thirty and went to the chow hall for lunch. The first briefing came a few hours later. The plan called for the tank platoon to spend the next few weeks in its area of operations with a cavalry unit from Fort Hood, Texas. The briefing focused on the outgoing unit’s counter-IED operations. Their tactics were described as unorthodox but effective. Insurgents were using houses in the platoon’s designated sector to prepare IEDs and the bombs were being placed at previous blast sites, presumably for the sake of expedience. Most common in the IED inventory was the victim-operated device, with phony “command wires” left in plain sight to draw the attention of American soldiers. It proved to be an effective enemy tactic, as troopers focused on phony IEDs were regularly stumbling into the kill zone of the real devices.

Intelligence reports suggested that bomb making materials were being transported in taxi cabs. The area of operations was Amiriya, which was predominantly Sunni, and from within that local population had sprung an uprising of al-Qaeda forces against the Shiite death squads that had destabilized the region. Military intelligence had determined that those al-Qaeda forces could be the closest thing to an ally the Americans were going to find. Trying to figure out who were the good guys in a festering conflict between al-Qaeda and bands of Shiite death squads committing genocide could make anyone's head spin, but the senior leaders broke it down after the meeting: They faced a growing insurgency and their mission was to push it out of their area of operations.

At Camp Liberty, much of the preparations resembled those in Kuwait. Endless hours of performing maintenance on vehicles, weapons and other equipment, occasionally interrupted by meals and sleep. The tank platoon received four armored Humvees in addition to its fleet of four tanks, and free time was limited. When free time was granted, downloading and watching pornography was routine for many. Fisher always said the Army looked the other way from soldiers watching pornography in violation of orders and the laws of the host nation because porn depicts treating people as objects and this enables a soldier to dehumanize the enemy. Joe suspected it was among Fisher's many conspiracy theories regarding the government. As for the platoon tent, it had been transformed into a maze of blankets and ponchos that were hung in every way imaginable, with each soldier constructing his own private shanty within which to go about his personal affairs.

The time to go outside the wire and start hunting drew near. Joe savored the growing intensity as the days passed. He believed in his Army training and equipment, and it gave him confidence. He watched a professional boxing bout with a soldier named Fisher Santana in a large, hangar-style building run by the Army's Morale, Welfare and Recreation department. Fisher was on his third tour in Iraq. He grew up in the Kensington neighborhood of North Philadelphia, one of the toughest parts of the city. His father was Sandy Santana, a Dominican, and his mother, Sarah, was an Irish girl from nearby Fishtown, and they named the last of their four sons in honor of her neighborhood against her father's wishes, which was to call him Sammy.

Fisher was born in the family home near the corner of Howard and Somerset streets. He was born at home because the street was blocked off by police investigating a murder that occurred in front of the two-story row house. The body was still on the street when Fisher made his way into the world. Fisher showed up fast. He was breathing on his own within thirty minutes from the time Sarah's water broke.

The fight on television was a championship bout between the welterweights Zab Judah and Miguel Cotto from Madison Square Garden. It was a rerun being shown on the Armed Forces Network.

"That Puerto Rican is a dirty fighter," Fisher said, referring to Cotto's punches below Judah's waistline.

"If you're gonna start talking shit about your hero, Guzmán, I'm gonna get and leave," Joe said. Fisher was a former amateur fighter, and he followed the top Dominican fighters of the day. His favorite was Joan Guzmán.

"Nah, bro. This was a good fight. Cotto deserved to win," Fisher said.

"Good, because I didn't get to see it too good yesterday with everybody acting stupid in here. I wanna break this fight down."

Fisher opened a pouch of Red Man chewing tobacco. He jammed his hand into the bag, looking for a plug to calm his nerves. Fisher was in his mid-thirties, nearly Joe's age.

"My daughter's going to a dance this week. I was talking to my wife, Leslie, about it last night," Fisher said, as he grabbed a pinch of chewing tobacco and put it in his mouth. "She got on her high boots and her beautiful little dress, and that purple hair she has now. My wife did her hair for her because she's in a sling from playing softball."

Joe nodded and reached into the bag Fisher offered, grabbing a pinch of moist tobacco leaves and putting it in his mouth.

"She can't do anything with her left hand," Fisher explained. She has a date with a girl named Paige."

"White girl name if I ever heard one."

"Whatever. Anyway, they're together and it's her first real date. My wife put her on the phone, and we had a conversation about two girls dancing, and I told her, hey, don't worry about anybody else because there's always going to be those people that are like, what the hell? Even in middle school, you know what I'm saying?

And there's bullies out there, so I had a conversation with her. Don't worry about it, block it out, dance with your girlfriend. Know what I'm saying? So that was good."

"Hey, man, that's all that matters if your daughter's happy. Who cares what other people think? Matter of fact, if you want to bring her to San Antonio when we get home, my mom and my sisters will throw her a quinceañera. It'll be nice, bro. She can bring her girlfriend, too. It's all good for you and your family down where I'm at, know what I'm saying?"

"Hey, that's from the chest, man. I appreciate it."

A soldier burst into the room. The platoon leader and platoon sergeant had called an emergency meeting outside the sleeping tent. Joe and Fisher hurried there, wondering what the urgency was about. The platoon was briefed on a change of mission. The company was going to be relocated within the vicinity of the Mansour district, but outside the area for which it had planned.

While Amiriya was largely Sunni, the newly designated area of operations, Al-Jami'ah, was mostly Shia. Once considered potential allies, the Sunni militants of al-Qaeda in Iraq were now the enemy, along with the Shia militia group, Jaysh al-Mahdi. Also known as JAM, it was not a designated terrorist organization, but an armed political faction vying for control of Iraq. Within the sector, JAM was conducting criminal activities and established itself as hostile toward coalition forces.

The platoon had barely arrived in Iraq, and the mission had already changed. As the mission changed, so did preparations. Focus turned to the Humvees, while the tanks were all but ignored. On the eve of the tank platoon's first venture outside the wire, it received a shipment of M240B machine guns. The belt-fed, gas-operated weapons were "medium" machine guns that featured buttstocks and could, if necessary, be dismounted from any platform, hand-carried into combat, and fired from the shoulder. They fired a 7.62mm round and, in the M240 "B" configuration, were common to infantry and scout units. Nobody in the platoon of tankers relished the idea of lugging around the weapons, each of which weighed twenty-seven pounds without ammunition.

Another late arrival was an assortment of radio equipment that had most of the tankers dumbfounded. The radios came with the trucks, but the increasingly frantic pace of pre-combat operations left them unattended until hours before the first trip outside the safety of Camp Liberty. Once they got their hands on the radio equipment, they struggled to get them to work.

The outgoing cavalry troopers that had been in the sector for months would be guiding the newcomers through the neighborhood. The start of the mission was delayed for more than an hour as everybody worked on the radio problem, and it was a supreme embarrassment for Joe's platoon. His rank as a lower enlisted soldier did not shield him from the shame. Upon finally getting communications established, they departed Camp Liberty at seven-thirty in the morning.

Joe was the driver of the lead truck in a column that consisted of five vehicles carrying twenty-one soldiers. Having waited almost six years since the terrorist attacks of September 11, 2001, Joe found himself behind the wheel of an armored Humvee in southwestern

Baghdad. Keeping in mind all the counter-IED procedures that had been learned and rehearsed over the past eighteen months, he scanned the road while driving the lead vehicle into the sector of responsibility. They traveled along a main route called Ratt. Standard operating procedure called for driving against the flow of traffic, which yielded to the Army vehicles out of self-preservation. The commander of Joe's truck was a senior non-commissioned officer from the accompanying unit acting as a guide.

They turned onto Route Phonecard and traversed a highway overpass toward what appeared to be an abandoned retail district. The road was about fifty meters in width and divided by a dirt median. Department stores and billboards lined both sides of the empty streets. The area resembled a post-apocalyptic nightmare. Trash was piled densely along the curbs and sidewalks. They passed a checkpoint manned by Iraqi soldiers every hundred or so meters.

After a few miles, they turned away from the business district into a residential neighborhood. They maneuvered the trucks through a maze of narrow streets, many of which were blocked by concrete barriers. Children were everywhere, running across the path of Joe's truck as they begged for candy. He tried to keep an eye on them while scanning for potential IEDs along the streets and curbsides. They approached a massive expanse of a vacant lot known as the Field of Death, then onward toward a chokepoint called The Gauntlet, where the road narrowed into a kill zone against previous American forces. The surrounding houses were lined with concrete walls and multiple-storied rooftops to create a paradise for snipers and IED triggermen.

The patrol stopped and the soldiers dismounted and entered a local school that had been converted into a security station manned by American soldiers and Iraqi police forces. It was the platoon's first visit to Joint Security Station (JSS) Medina, a compound three stories in height and nestled within a residential neighborhood. The visit was brief as senior members of the platoon met with their counterparts and, as they departed the compound, gunfire broke out a short distance away, most likely warning shots by Iraqi Army or police. The patrol took them to a roundabout within the district. In the morning daylight, Joe saw a human skull and leg bones in the middle of the road. There was a ribcage on a nearby sidewalk. The area was devoid of living people.

They stopped and marked the area using a Global Positioning System. The sergeant sitting next to Joe said the information would be turned over to the Iraqi Army. Somebody in the truck asked if they might compel the Iraqi soldiers to recover the human remains. The sergeant said that if they were to do so, the Iraqis would only laugh at them. Stray dogs would eat most of the remains and drag the bones away, he mentioned offhandedly. Joe sat in the truck and brooded over the soldier's attitude toward death. He considered the gravity of the man's words, which were voiced in such a casual manner.

Who are we looking for? The thought came upon him as it had before. Swept up in his youth by stories in books he read about the Texas Rangers, the early American lawmen beset on many sides by Indian fighters, Mexican bandidos, and lawbreakers of every ilk, and added to that, the struggle to survive the environment of the untamed, American West.

Every story needs a bad guy. The bad guys in this case were ghosts. All Joe was told was that they hated Americans. All the evidence scattered around the traffic circle left no doubt the enemy was active in that area. Piles of bones sitting in the hot sun as casual as a package of mail on a doorstep, too large to stuff into the recipient's door slot.

Such reasoning gave him a headache. He recalled the stories from his youth of the Mexican bandit Juan Cortina. The Red Robber of the Rio Grande swore that Anglo-Saxon settlers in Mexico would not possess the land until they had fed the soil with their own blood. Joe was resentful of the anger rising within him, being distracted at such a critical moment. An IED triggerman was out there somewhere, waiting for an American patrol to wander along.

4

The platoon moved from Camp Liberty to JSS Medina. Tankers packed their individual equipment into the Humvees at the FOB and brought it to Medina. The strategy of living among the locals and applying pressure to the Iraq insurgency had begun.

Soldiers remounted the trucks for a patrol with added manpower from the Texas cavalry troop. The truck column stopped in the middle of the street next to a fruit and vegetable stand. Across the street sat a vacant, three-story brick building, its façade collapsed into a heap of rubble that covered the sidewalk and part of the street.

The platoon leader was a second lieutenant from Mississippi named Elijah Redd. The young officer's voice came over the radio, giving an order to dismount the vehicles and search the damaged building. Joe had been replaced as a driver, having volunteered to be one of the soldiers that would be on foot, seeking out the enemy. After watching videos of Humvees being blown apart during the two weeks of preparations in Kuwait, he figured he would take his chances as a foot soldier. After all, he had joined the Army with the intent of shooting a terrorist in the face, and he wasn't likely to get the opportunity sitting behind the steering wheel of a truck.

He stepped out of the truck and onto the street. His hands trembled as he gripped his M16 rifle and the platoon set up outside the damaged building. Most of the structures that packed the narrow street were multiple-story houses, and he scanned the windows and rooftops for people. Counter-sniper tactics ran through his mind as he moved quickly amid the cover of trees and cars that lined the road. He had a lapse of concentration as he recalled something written by Sun Tzu…

Do not linger in dangerously isolated positions.

Angered by the distraction, he kept moving around the perimeter of the building, maintaining security while soldiers entered and searched the interior.

The patrol attracted the attention of local civilians, who emerged from their houses and watched the activity. Vehicle traffic stopped several blocks away in either direction, giving the platoon a buffer zone to work in while searching. They had been told earlier the Iraqi people were keenly aware of the unit insignia on Army uniforms. As time went by since the invasion four years beforehand, American soldiers bearing different patches on their sleeves had come and gone, and the arrival of a new unit was noticed by everyone, both civilians and insurgents. Joe stayed outside the building, picking his way from one covered position to another every few moments to make things difficult for any sniper that might have been in the vicinity.

As curious onlookers watched, he was aware that life was marked not by minutes, but by every breath taken. If he were killed by a sniper or a bomb, it was possible he would not feel anything. On the street, in the daytime heat and constant danger, he thought of his wife and sons. The distraction irked him as he hunkered under the narrow shade of a palm tree and tried to make himself a challenging target for the enemy. He found himself staring across the street at a cardboard box overflowing with bananas, swarmed with flies under the glare of the sun. His brain boiled in the summer heat while attempting to process the sensory overload.

Sweat seeped out of his body and drenched his uniform. The search team emerged from the building. They had not found anything. Soldiers remounted the vehicles and made their way to an affluent neighborhood, where massive, ornate homes sat behind high walls and iron gates. Many of them were abandoned, and one of them was selected for search and they dismounted. Once again, he was on the street, staying close to cover. He suddenly noticed a staff sergeant from his platoon standing within arm's reach, and Joe abandoned the safety of his position to look for another.

"Where are you going?" the staff sergeant asked.

"Away from you," Joe told him, angered that he had gotten too close to him, possibly making them a target for the enemy.

Elsewhere on the street, soldiers stood together in small groups. Joe's nerves were in a jangled state. He gripped his rifle more tightly as a flush of irritation welled within him. The platoon was asking for trouble, becoming complacent already. It was late in the afternoon and he was drenched. His uniform and body armor were getting heavier by each moment, and the constant efforts to move quickly and seek cover had worn him down. He slumped against a wall on the shady side of the street. After a few moments he was moving again, up and down the sidewalk hurriedly, occasionally moving to the street to take cover by the trucks.

A crackle of gunfire sent everyone running for cover. It came from close by, perhaps a block at most. On the street corner, he took a knee against a wall. Lieutenant Redd stood a few paces away, using his radio to reposition the trucks. Moments passed as Joe's brain teetered between dread and excitement. Nothing happened. They maintained a defensive posture as the search team came out of the building and everyone got back into the trucks.

The patrol continued in what amounted to not much more than driving around for a while. Shortly after six o'clock in the afternoon, they finished the patrol and went back to the Medina compound. The platoon conducted a review of the mission that just occurred, whereupon they were told by the platoon leadership that the security station would probably be their home in Iraq for the next fifteen months.

The tankers occupied the first floor of the building. The living area was an open bay, with black, tiled floors, and walls painted powder blue. There was a central air-conditioning system, but several of the windows were broken and sheets of cardboard had been used to patch the damage. About a dozen portable toilets were at the compound, which was home to more than one hundred Army soldiers and their Iraqi counterparts. There was a rancid smell outside the toilets as the feces marinated in the summer heat.

A spare room was crudely fashioned into a gym with a bench and some weightlifting equipment. The whitewashed walls were barren except for a black-and-white photograph of a young Arnold Schwarzenegger. Machine-gun emplacements were situated on top of the third-story roof. Each fighting position was a bunker of sandbags and camouflage nets and stocked with hundreds of rounds of machine-gun ammunition and a few AT4 recoilless rifles. The entrance of the compound was an open archway, and it was blocked by an armored personnel carrier. Concrete barriers were placed in the road leading to the walled compound, creating a serpentine that forced approaching vehicles to slow down.

Joe's first night at the station passed without sleep. He stood a guard shift on the rooftop for six hours. It started at midnight in a bunker facing east. Sporadic gunfire interrupted the night, but none of it was directed at the compound. Fisher showed up in the middle of the shift with a handful of cold Rip It energy drinks.

"Hey man, you awake in there?" Fisher asked, standing outside the sandbagged bunker. Joe stepped out, then stood up straight and stretched, which was impossible inside the cramped bunker. He took one of the energy drinks, walked to the chest-high ledge of the rooftop, and laid his M16 rifle across it.

"What got you pissed off out there today?" Fisher said. "Briggs told me something happened but didn't go into details. He just said Cuero is mad, bro."

"Fuck, man. That idiot of a section sergeant was standing right next to me when we were on the street earlier today."

Fisher burst into laughter. "I knew it had to be that guy!" he said, cracking open a can of Rip It and taking a sip. "The last time we were here, we were set up on an IED, waiting for hours for EOD to show up, as usual. We're sitting in the tank, looking around, you know, and he turns to me and says, get your NVDs and look for a heat signature for that IED. And I'm like, what a stupid fuck. I had to explain to him NVDs work off ambient light, they're not thermal optics. Can you believe that shit? He got all pissed off and started talking shit about giving me an Article 15 for disrespecting an NCO, and I'm like, whatever. Go ahead and write it up how you told me to look for a heat signature with NVDs and the platoon sergeant will laugh in your face, motherfucker."

Joe shook his head and stared into the dark neighborhood surrounding JSS Medina. Nothing out there was moving.

"You hear from your wife?" asked Joe.

"Yeah. She's working on us going to D.R. when I get back. The trip is almost three grand, so it'll be two-hundred dollars a month until then. I'm like, damn, that's another bill. We've been talking about it, and with my daughter getting ready to be in high school soon, we're trying to set money aside for college. And she's getting ready for cheer camp. She's excited. So that was pretty much it. I got something to eat and went to sleep, but I woke up because Briggs was playing his Patti LaBelle music loud on his laptop again. What's with that dude and Patti LaBelle? I ain't never seen no white boy into soul music as much as that kid."

"Don't get me started about Briggs."

"Ah, whatever. Anyway, since I couldn't go back to sleep, I figured you might need a Rip It."

"Thanks," Joe said. "You know, I was serious about what we were talking about before, when your daughter turns fifteen, and bringing her down to Texas for her quinceañera. She might have to leave her girlfriend in Philly, now that I've had time to think of it. They're not ready for that in San Antonio, man."

Fisher laughed at the thought. "Yeah, bro, bet. You got your Rip It. You good up here?"

"Yeah, I'll make it. Try to get some sleep. Probably got a busy day coming up."

"Don't forget your NVDs. See if you got any heat signatures out there," Fisher said, walking away.

"That fucking guy," Joe said, crawling back into the bunker.

Dawn approached toward the end of his shift, and an apparition appeared on the horizon. It was the brooding hulk of the great Al-Rahman Mosque, moored to the past of Saddam Hussein's defeated empire. Abandoned cranes were perched around the sprawling edifice of the main dome and the smaller domes that sat around it. The mosque sat there in the morning haze, frozen in the orbit of history.

5

Moments after Joe's guard shift ended, the platoon embarked on a mission to find a mosque and its imam. His arms and legs were already heavy with fatigue when the Humvees stopped on a residential street and the soldiers dismounted. The area was dead quiet, and the only sound he heard as he studied the surroundings was a dull, ringing sensation in his ears.

An elderly woman emerged from a house and approached him. She invited him into her home, but he declined as politely as possible. The woman spoke English well, so he asked her if she had seen any bad guys around. No, she replied, and offered him a bottle of water. He again declined an offer of hospitality from the old woman. Gunfire was heard a few nights prior on the busy street, the woman said, and he was encouraged by her willingness to provide information.

A language barrier arose when he asked her where to find the nearest mosque, and where the imam might be at that hour of the morning. The conversation with the woman caught the attention of the platoon sergeant. Sergeant First Class Maurice Young was a thickly muscled, career enlisted man from Stone Mountain, Georgia. Young took over the conversation with the woman and asked her about the mosque and its imam.

At a nearby corner, Joe was approached by another woman who appeared to be middle aged. She seemed to understand English well and they talked about the neighborhood, which she said had been quiet for about a month. Her English fluency faltered as soon as Joe mentioned the mosque and its leader. She abruptly excused herself and hurried away.

The Baja Company commander, Captain Zach Davis, joined the morning patrol. He and several of the senior members of the platoon turned their attention to an abandoned house with a locked gate, but their interest quickly wore off, and they decided against climbing the gate for a closer look. The soldiers returned to the trucks and headed for the northern end of the sector, which was more volatile than the south according to the intel reports. Once there, they went through The Gauntlet, and an area known as the Dog Bone, in a show of defiance to the hidden enemy, daring them to come out for a fight. The patrol remained quiet as they drove around the streets for three hours before returning to JSS Medina.

Upon arrival, they downloaded their gear. Joe offered Fisher a Newport, and they stood under the shade of a compound wall to smoke cigarettes.

"These patrols are a grind," Joe said, lighting a Newport. "It's like listening to the P.L. giving one of his college lectures about the social contract theory or some shit."

"Yeah, I know," Fisher said. "I would rather be out there on patrol than listen to him talking about Rousseau."

Joe laughed. "Or how about Tommy Hobbes, or John Locke and the clean slate, maybe? That's gonna last until next year, you're gonna be here regurgitating Gordon Wood."

"Don't remind me," Fisher said, holding a puff a smoke from the cigarette before letting it drift out of his nostrils. "These patrols, it's like spending all day in the woods hunting, not seeing a damn thing. Then the day ends with stepping in bear shit."

"You do a lot of hunting in Philly?"

"You got jokes, Manny. Naw, upstate. In the mountains. I been hunting all my life."

Fisher called people Manny when he got worked up in conversation. He called almost everyone Manny. "My dad would take off work from his factory job and take me hunting upstate every year since I was old enough to go when I was twelve. My first time out, we went deer hunting. We used to go upstate to Cameron County. You know they got elk up there? Anyway, the first time out, I had a Marlin thirty-thirty my dad bought me for my birthday, and I had to wait almost a year while he took me to a gun range outside Philly, shooting and getting it sighted in. We're up in the woods on a ridgeline and I'm looking down when the sun is just coming up, and I see a mama racoon dragging her baby up into a tree and putting it in the hole. When that happened, I don't know, I knew I could never pull the trigger on an animal and feel good about it. I was just done, you know?"

"You went hunting every year? You never told me that. All you ever told me about was growing up in the streets."

"Yeah, every year. We went fishing in the spring and summer. When summer was over and school started again, we went hunting."

"You ever shoot anything?"

"Yeah, sometimes. Squirrels, rabbits, woodchucks. I always felt like shit when I did, though. My dad was into that stuff, though.

He said we had Cherokee in our blood. Whenever we killed something, he would go to it and run his hand over it, like he was petting it. That shit hit me every time, but I tried not to let him see me cry."

"I dig that. He was showing respect."

"Yeah. He was deep like that. When we shot something, he said it was a gift. I don't know if he was trying to make me feel better or what. It made my chest feel tight. I saw that shit in a movie, where this kid was drinking a deer's blood, you know? That was bullshit."

"I'm thinking of the parasites that could be in the blood, for one thing."

"Right, anyway, I could never do that shit, Manny. My dad never did that shit. When we killed something, I just wanted to go home. I loved being out there in the woods and in the fields. I loved it. No matter how cold or how tired I was, I loved it. We never went turkey hunting, though. You got to be dressed like Special Forces to hunt those motherfuckers."

"Yeah, no shit. I know guys who hunt them in Texas. They got eyes like binoculars. You can't fuck with turkeys unless you're damn near invisible."

After lunch they went back out with Captain Davis riding in one of the trucks. The company commander seemed to be taking an interest in his bastard platoon of tankers. They returned to the abandoned, gated house from the earlier patrol, but this time with bolt cutters. A search of the building revealed thick layers of dust everywhere, so it seemed nobody had lived there for a long time.

They discovered fresh footprints and a handful of passports laid on a table that had been wiped clear of the dust.

The discovery lifted the spirits of the search team, and the documents were collected for further analysis by intelligence officials back at Camp Liberty. The find suggested that, at the very least, criminal activity was taking place in their sector.

Passports were stashed for safe keeping in one of the trucks, and the soldiers embarked on a foot patrol of a street nearby. A market lined up on one side of the road, but something was wrong. During the truck patrol earlier in the day, the street bustled with people shopping the rows of stores. The shops were closed upon the platoon's return, the doors padlocked, and not a soul was seen anywhere. A group of boys motioned for the soldiers to come to them, eager to tell something. Tension bubbled among the soldiers. Before they could talk to the boys, a gunner in a nearby Humvee started shouting at Captain Davis. One of the infantry platoons was at the Field of Death, and some of his soldiers had been hit by small-arms fire.

They climbed back into the trucks and raced toward the skirmish. Radio contact was made with White Platoon, which was rushing its wounded back to Camp Liberty. The sound of gunfire greeted the tank platoon as it sped toward the scene. Up ahead, Iraqi soldiers took cover at a checkpoint. They were under enemy fire as the American truck column roared through, tracer fire zipping by in different directions. The Iraqis returned fire toward buildings and rooftops, but from the safety of the trucks the American soldiers could not see enemy fighters as they pushed through the firefight.

Tracer rounds whizzed past the trucks and the drivers pushed gas pedals to the floorboards, swerving through the shootout and careening around corners, onward toward their destination, leaving the Iraqi soldiers to their gunfight.

Upon arrival at the Field of Death, the tankers linked up with Blue Platoon, which had hastily mounted their trucks at JSS Medina and rushed to the site of the attack on White Platoon, which had been attacked while conducting a foot patrol. The blood of Baja Company had been spilled, and it was time for the local population to pay the price, Joe was sure of that. He could see the same look on the faces of the other soldiers in his platoon.

Somewhere near the crossroads of Army doctrine and conventional wisdom, the conclusion was that the locals assuredly knew what was going on in their neighborhood, and their failure to bring that knowledge to the Americans would have its consequences. The American troops had run out of patience with subtle tactics. Two teams rapidly assembled in the aftermath of the attack, with the first squad tasked with clearing buildings and the other conducting a thorough search.

A city block was sealed off by Humvees stationed at intersections, and soldiers moved swiftly to get the operation underway. Everything happened so quickly that Joe dismounted his truck and found himself a block away from a group of soldiers already running around a corner toward its objective. With known enemy presence in the area, he struck out in pursuit of his team as fast as he could run. When he rounded the corner where he had last seen them, they were nowhere in sight. Joe was alone and on foot, and the truck he had dismounted had left to take up another position. There was neither an American soldier or vehicle in sight, and he was in the middle of Baghdad moments after an attack on American soldiers.

He started running again. The prospect of going back the way he had come was not an option, because if a sniper had seen him the first time he had run down the street, he did not want to risk another opportunity. His mind raced to make decisions in microseconds as he ran at full speed down the street in broad daylight, then rounded a corner and almost collided into a pack of soldiers. Out of breath, he sank down onto one knee and gulped water from his canteen. He was smoked from exhaustion, and they had not begun the search-and-clear mission.

The clearing team breached a house occupied by a man, his wife, and several small children. Joe was part of the follow-on search squad. A sergeant leading the way told them to ransack the house, which was a well-kept, three-story home. Joe started in a living room on the ground floor, digging through the seat cushions of a sofa. Under Iraqi law, each household was allowed one rifle and as much as fifty rounds of ammunition. When the soldiers entered the house, they found an AK-47 rifle atop a kitchen stove. Within moments of the search, a shout came from another room on the first floor. A second AK-47 had been found under a pile of rugs.

The sergeant leading the search snarled an order. "Tear this place apart. They're already in trouble, so fuck 'em."

Joe took several photographs of the rifles. The sounds of soldiers searching the house grew louder. A pack mentality settled in, but no words were spoken. They went from room to room, sending carboard boxes, rugs, and clothes flying in every direction. They found a cellphone and confronted the man, who had said he did not own one. The phone was photographed, as were a handful of shotgun shells found in an empty room on the second floor.

They departed without detaining the man, who seemed to take it in stride as soldiers turned his home upside down. He offered them water as they confiscated his weapons. A small boy screamed at the soldiers as they left the home. His mother tried to hush his outburst, but to no avail. His voice carried across a courtyard in front of the house as they stepped into the sweltering afternoon heat.

The mission to search and clear the area continued through several houses but yielded nothing. Tired and exhausted by the heat, Joe got back into a truck. The mission was called off at about four-thirty, and they went back to Medina, where they got word that none of the injured soldiers had been seriously hurt. A debriefing of all three platoons revealed that a white sedan had been following their patrols since Baja Company had arrived. It was clear that someone had been shadowing the company like a ghost, and that the attack that occurred was not a random act, but a calculated strike.

The soldiers did not give the enemy the honor of calling them insurgents. To the Americans, they were shitheads. That was what soldiers called them. They had spilled American blood first, but the soldiers were going to be around for a long time. The shitheads could not hide forever.

6

Joe had awakened from a nightmare. In his dream, a Humvee disappeared in an explosion, with dull waves of debris and grit descending from the sky in the aftermath. The truck was hit by an IED. Daylight was shrouded in smoke from the blast of the bomb as he sprang from his truck. He aimed his rifle at women and children fleeing in panic, and he screamed toward them as they ran, but all he could hear was silence.

The voice of one of his college professors echoed in the darkness.

"The Apache Wars showed how cunning the Indian tribes were, even against the tactics of the Texas Rangers and cavalry soldiers."

From the gloom of the smoke stepped General George Crook. Joe studied the American general of the Indian Wars when he was a schoolboy in Texas. Seeing the old man in his weathered Civil War uniform unsettled him.

They're not going to forgive and forget if you let the old man get killed out here.

Joe had no idea what to say. The danger was everywhere.

"There's land for sale near Sonora, sir. We could find you a hundred acres and it wouldn't cost much. It's in the hill country."

The general had a look in his eyes that would not betray his thoughts. He gazed at Joe for a spell while soldiers swarmed the truck looking for survivors, but the doors would not open. It was all the courage Joe could muster to walk to where the old man was standing and try to convince him to move to a safer position. "We should really get off the street, sir."

Joe's Olds Cutlass from high school was parked at a nearby curb and beckoned the general.

"Sir, if you want, I can take you up to the hill country and then I'll come back."

General Crook walked slowly around the car, looking at it with a grimace on his face. Joe popped the latch under the hood and raised it. Underneath was a polished engine, everything chrome and black. It was the 502-cubic-inch motor Joe wanted when he bought the car when he turned sixteen. The car had been parked on his street his entire life until he bought it for five hundred dollars. The car was a piece of junk, but Joe spent almost as much money on solvents, degreasers and polish as he did for the ownership title and he worked hard to make it look new. And it did. He cruised the streets along Commerce and Buena Vista streets on the West Side of San Antonio all the way to downtown, then north up Broadway to where the rich kids lived in Alamo Heights.

Joe smiled, looking into the immaculate engine bay and the big-block motor inside.

Fuck this goddamn place. I want to go home.

Joe caught himself, then glanced at the general. He was stooped over at the waist, inspecting the engine. Finally, he straightened upright and closed the hood.

"There's no time," the general said, "my report from the field is due."

Hope for getting the general away from danger ebbed out of Joe. He searched his mind for another way out. They walked into a vacant building that looked like it had been used for selling appliances and electronics. Advertisement flyers for merchandise were stacked in piles on the dusty floor. Otherwise, the building was empty. General Crook hunched down and sorted through one of the stacks. Joe set aside his rifle and did the same, rummaging through ads for computers, hard drives, memory sticks, motherboards, power supplies, and video graphics cards. He wasn't sure what else to do.

We're gonna be late and they'll leave without us.

Time seemed to move faster than his mind could keep track. The next thing he knew, he and the general were back outside in the street, and the platoon had moved a few blocks away. A soldier covered in blood was placed into one of the Humvees. They were going to take him back to Camp Liberty and try to save his life. Joe had been there a thousand times in his mind, imagining such a moment, but his brain went blank as he tried to grasp the countless battle drills that had been rehearsed.

Vehicles from other units began to congregate around the platoon and its injured soldier. Soldiers checked on others who were in the truck that had been hit. They seemed to be okay. The gathering occurred in a haze of voices. He began to emerge from the dull stupor. Everyone remounted their trucks and headed back toward JSS Medina. Joe looked out the window. The general sat at a small table while eating a bacon, lettuce, and tomato sandwich while drinking a strawberry milkshake.

Wake up and get ready.

Joe awoke in the darkness of the tent at Camp Liberty. Alarm clocks were whirring and chirping. It was time to start another day.

"Get the fuck up."

It was Staff Sergeant Badger. He seemed obsessed with the sleep habits of the lower enlisted soldiers. As soon as he saw somebody lay down, he told them to get up. Upon waking, soldiers could count on seeing that loathsome expression on Badger's face, his eyes glaring down at them in disapproval. Badger was a New Jersey cop before joining the Army. He joined the Army before Desert Storm ended. Combat footage he had seen on television intrigued him, and he envisioned himself as a leader in the wartime Army. Before long he found himself on peacekeeping duty in The Balkans. Badger never fired a shot, but the experience quickened his desires even further. For nearly ten years he waited for his chance at combat, all the while moving up the ranks. He applied himself strenuously to be better than his peers.

It worked. Badger quickly established himself as a highly disciplined soldier. He studied Field Manual 7-22.7, The Army Noncommissioned Officer Guide. When the war on terrorism began after September 11, 2001, he was ready. As one of the dogface soldiers of the 3rd Infantry Division, he participated in the Thunder Run into Baghdad. The daring rush through the enemy's lines fed his impulsive yearnings. It was a "weapons free" environment in which American forces were authorized to use lethal force any time they felt threatened. Badger was a staff sergeant and tank commander, with the authority to order his crew to kill enemy fighters that swarmed about on foot and in vehicles during manic, sometimes freakish skirmishes that were a blur of gunfire and explosions. He returned two years later in 2005 for another grueling tour, and he was back once again.

“Cuero, get your ass in gear. You want to be a leader, start acting like one. You wanna get promoted to sergeant, but you’re in bed just like everybody else.”

Joe quickly donned his uniform as Badger berated him. “Roger, staff sergeant.”

“Stop saying roger and fucking get it done,” Badger snapped and walked out of the tent.

The sleep tent had enough bunk beds for an infantry platoon, so there was more than enough room for the tank platoon to spread out. Joe reached into a metal locker and pulled out his personal hygiene kit before going to the latrine. He wiped the condensation from a mirror and began shaving. At his side stood Briggs, wearing a towel around his waist and combing his freshly shampooed hair.

“Güero, if you get any bigger …”

“Yeah, I know,” Briggs grinned. “Where’s your amigo?”

“Fuck if I know.” He wasn’t in charge of Fisher, who had been to Iraq enough times that he could stay in his sleeping bag a little past wakeup and get away with it. Joe brushed his teeth and headed for the showers. “Did you leave any hot water?”

Briggs laughed and headed out the door.

After getting cleaned up, Joe put on his uniform and went to breakfast with his platoon mates. There was nothing better downrange than eating a meal in the chow hall. As soon he arrived in Kuwait, Joe was impressed by how much the food improved. Briggs and Fisher talked about how good it was going to be for over a year while in Georgia, but Joe suspected they were messing with him. Once in Kuwait, it was obvious they were telling the truth. Breakfast was the best meal of the day, prepared by mysterious Gambians able to whip up a quality Denver omelet within minutes. With hash browns and a cup of coffee, and Joe nearly thought he was back home.

"We got mail today," Fisher said as he plunked down into a chair next to Joe. "You know what that means?"

"Yeah, more of that smelly cologne you're always wearing," Briggs said.

Fisher placed his elbows on the table and looked at Briggs, who was sitting directly across from him and opening a carton of milk. "My man," Fisher said, "you've been to just two places in your life. That's Oklahoma, and this shithole right here, so I don't expect you to have an appreciation for the finer things in life. And another thing. It's not cologne, it's fragrance. Most of it you can't pronounce anyway."

Joe took entertainment from the banter between Fisher and Briggs. The more nobody said anything to break it up, the more they would go at each other. Outside the wire, they were thick as thieves.

“No shit, we got work to do this morning, so hurry up and eat,” Sergeant First Class Young said. Never had Joe met someone from the south with such a gruff manner. Everything about the platoon sergeant was glum. Rumor was, nobody had ever seen the man smile.

After breakfast, the soldiers went to the motor pool, located adjacent to the sleeping tents. They worked on the trucks under the heat and dust of a typical June morning in Iraq. It was hot. Soldiers laughed and cursed. They smoked cigarettes and stuffed wads of smokeless tobacco into their mouths, spitting slurries of brown goop into the sand between stories of back home, cars they were going to fix up, or had, and girls they had conquered. The men of the lower enlisted ranks turned wrenches while older, more experienced sergeants walked about, supervising, lending counsel and advice, yelling occasionally.

It was maintenance day downrange, suddenly broken by the shrill pierce of an alarm, incoming mortar fire! Tools were dropped and soldiers ran with urgency to concrete bunkers or crawled under the nearest vehicle. Off in the distance, a muffled *whump* where the round landed, then it was back to working on the vehicles as if nothing of significance had happened. Perhaps nobody was hurt, or there was a human being out there somewhere, blood spurting from a limb blown off by an enemy mortar round, dying in the sand.

They worked on their trucks all morning. The platoon sergeant walked about his group of soldiers, from one vehicle to the next. He knew the Army Noncommissioned Officer Guide like a minister knew the Holy Bible. Sergeant First Class Young could tell his soldiers about Percival Lowe, and many others from the pages of Army history, known for their discipline and valor. Whether keeping a horse or Humvee, an Abrams tank or just about anything else that traveled on wheels or tracks, they were altogether in for this one.

The present was not a time for reasoning, but the execution phase of everything for which they had prepared and sacrificed. They were going to lose men on this tour of duty, just as he had seen in the past. His men were ready. They would not be betrayed by a lack of training. It was the soldier's training and equipment that would keep him alive or betray him at a moment of authenticity, when one man sought to kill another man.

Young joined the post-Vietnam Army in 1991, well into the transition back to a volunteer force that started in the late seventies. He saw his first combat as a tank driver during Desert Storm. He helped liberate Kuwait, then spent the following ten years getting ready for the next big one. Young believed a soldier was developed through education, training, and experience, which he did his best to impart upon his platoon. Nothing could duplicate the experience they were embarking upon, and he was accountable for every man in the platoon.

"Get those tools put up," Young barked at his soldiers. "It's time for lunch."

7

It had been a few weeks since the first time outside the wire. Soldiers got picked off by small-arms fire and IEDs, but they were from other platoons. Word of mouth carried the news, finding out somebody you knew had been hit. The truth about what happened was a blur, even for those who were there and witnessed it. Everybody had their own facts and images in their heads about how it went down, but that didn't help those who weren't there. Somebody they knew was gone, just like that, and it would never make sense.

Then Baja Company was hit. An infantry platoon shot up in a drive-by, then hit by an IED as it evacuated the wounded. No additional information was given to those who called in to help. As part of the response, Joe's platoon established a security cordon near the blast site, only to realize they had rolled over a suspected secondary IED in the road on their way in. Explosive Ordnance Disposal was called to the scene and confirmed everyone's suspicions. They detonated the secondary IED the platoon had rolled past, as well as a third, tertiary bomb just fifteen meters from that device.

Joe waited in the back of a Humvee while the EOD techs prepared to detonate the twin bombs. Fisher sat next to him. They had earned the reputation of being the tank platoon's best door kickers in previous weeks, when the patrols led them to vacant buildings in search of enemy personnel, weapons caches, and bomb-making materials.

As they watched the sun rise, it was clear the insurgents had become more active in setting IEDs. Raids in recent days turned up infrared cameras, computers, and satellite phones, which left no doubt the enemy in Al-Jami'ah was not only clever and effective, but he was also well-funded and technically proficient.

All the evidence was found without any assistance from the civilians in the area, who never missed an opportunity to claim they knew nothing of activity in their neighborhoods that suggested the presence of insurgents or criminals. Joe sat in the Humvee and mulled it over, feeling more frustrated as the minutes passed. The streets were quiet, except for the growl of the truck's engine as it idled.

"You ever go to church?" Joe asked Fisher.

"Of course. My mom was Irish Catholic, and my dad was Dominican, Manny."

"I was an altar boy for a while," Joe said. "I used to sit there while Father said mass, and I looked out into the pews and saw people's faces I just wanted to smash in. They had such smug looks on their faces. I'm getting that feeling lately, talking to these people who smile, but never know shit about anything, and there's an IED on every corner lately."

"Welcome to Iraq. You wanna fuck somebody up right now, Manny? This is my third time over here. Wait until you been here some more. It's gonna get worse."

After EOD set off both bombs, the platoon dismounted for a foot patrol. The soldiers found a strand of copper wire at one of the blast sites and traced it to an abandoned schoolhouse. Once inside, they discovered a triggerman's hideout and the initiator for an IED. Perhaps the triggerman had fled after the first bomb had detonated. The platoon that was hit suffered a few scrapes and bruises but otherwise walked away healthy.

Joe's platoon had yet to make any significant contact with the enemy other than sporadic gunfire that sent soldiers running for cover and got the blood pumping faster. The enemy stayed invisible, never in the open for the Americans to engage. It had become a frustrating routine that persisted as the days of June passed, temperatures soared, and insurgents maintained their phantom presence.

A week passed before Joe realized he had not called his wife. A trip to Camp Liberty for resupply gave him the opportunity. Once he had his wife on the phone, there was uncomfortable disconnect. Her voice sounded different. He had no reason to suspect she was messing around. They had been married almost ten years before he joined the Army, and they had eyes only for each other ever since.

Hearing his wife's voice after a week chasing shadows, it was like she was a different person from his past, like every other girl he had known. This was his beloved, and the strange feeling inside him was unlike anything he had ever experienced. He preferred enemy tracer rounds zipping past his head to hearing her voice at that moment, so he made up an excuse to end the conversation and went back to the motor pool to get ready for the next patrol. Fisher and Briggs were there, as usual, wearing coveralls smothered in grease and dust. The sun was beating down. Soldiers took breaks every few minutes to guzzle water from plastic bottles. They wanted nothing more than to finish working on their vehicles and return to the shade and darkness of the sleeping tents before returning to their home at Medina, even with the smell of feces penetrating the building's musty interior.

A small group of new privates were inside the tent, cleaning their rifles. Joe ignored the fresh meat, slumped onto his bed and closed his eyes, waiting for sleep. The soldiers talked over each other in a chatter that sounded like it was far away, as did the clink and clunk of metal on metal while they cleaned their weapons.

"They did a ruck march around the track and he just fell out."

"That's kind of sad."

"The first ruck march I did was super easy. It was funny."

"I missed my first ruck march because I was sick. I had to go to sick call to see that muscle guy, what do you call him? Anyway, I go to him because I dislocated my shoulder. It was in combatives. I didn't want to give up. We just kept going and we had a chance to go for the streamer. We just kept going at it and going at it, and he got me in an arm bar, so I twisted around and popped my shoulder out of the way and put him in a choke hold. I won but it hurt, and I had to go and get it put back into place."

Abruptly their voices were cut short by the boom of the platoon sergeant, as Sergeant First Class Young interrupted them. "I need two men for a detail, now!"

A scuffle of boots running toward the voice died down, and the tent fell silent again. After a few moments, Joe sensed the presence of somebody else in the tent.

"Who's over there?" he asked.

"I'm the new guy. One of the new guys, sir."

"Don't call me sir. I work for a living." Joe jumped from the bed and swept aside the bed sheet that made for the door of his enclosure. He saw a private sitting on a wood crate and holding a rifle he was cleaning. Joe glared at the soldier and considered him without moving his eyes. The kid looked like he was right out of high school, but it was early summer, so he was likely a dropout. He could not have graduated and gone through basic training already. Perhaps he just appeared young for his age.

"Where you from?" Joe asked.

"Arizona."

"Yeah? Where in Arizona?"

"Twin Arrows."

"You the hero with the dislocated shoulder?"

"Yes, specialist."

"Alright private, let's step outside for a minute." With the prospect of sleep broken, Joe decided to size up the new guy before Fisher and Briggs got to him. The way Joe saw it, he was doing the kid a favor.

"How about telling me how the story ends," Joe said, hunching down on a metal folding chair outside the tent.

"The story?"

"Yeah, with your dislocated shoulder."

"Oh, right," the private said, reaching out to accept a Newport that Joe offered. "I was on profile for a couple days after that."

"Boy, I bet that sucked."

"Yes, specialist. They told me to do stretches for a couple days. That was the only time I didn't do P.T. or anything like that. I didn't miss anything, thank God. They were recycling people for missing stuff. Like if you had a profile and they were throwing grenades or something, and you missed the training, you know?"

"Yeah, I know."

"But at the same time, they were pushing to get people over here, giving them waivers. Some people who were out of shape, stuff like that. Basic training was bullshit, if you don't mind me saying."

"Don't talk about that around here, okay? Our platoon sergeant was a drill sergeant, for one thing. As for another thing, well, don't talk about that, alright?"

"Okay, specialist, thanks. I forget where I was. It's so fucking hot here. There was something else that fucked people up in basic."

"Land nav?"

"No."

"Grenades?"

"No."

"Rifle marksmanship?"

"No."

"You know most of basic is just to test how the drill sergeants are doing, right?"

"So, it's not about us passing or failing?"

"Yes and no. What do you think?"

"I remember taking a test. It was like, get one question wrong and you're being recycled. I was like, I made it this far and you're going to send me back for some book test? For getting an answer wrong. I was confused."

"I know what you mean. It's all head games. When I was going through, we had a strong platoon, but it was a stupid platoon at the same time. We went to the range, zeroed our rifles, went back to the range the next day, and nobody could hit shit. Turns out, our drill sergeants had messed up our sights that night, just to fuck with us maybe, who knows. They might have thought we were smarter or better than we were, like they had a side bet with the other drill sergeants, or it was supposed to be a teaching moment. There were a few that qualified with their weapons that day, the rest of us failed and got recycled. But all of us are still over here, so what difference did it make, right?"

"Right," the kid said, finishing his cigarette. "Not to change the subject, but I'm freaking out over the radios. Can you help me with that?"

Joe leaned back in his chair and paused. The new guy appeared to be Hispanic, but there was something different about him. Maybe the Arizona sun had a different effect, Joe wasn't sure about it.

"You said you're from Two Guns?"

"No, Twin Arrows. Kind of the next town over, but I'm not from town."

"You part Indian?"

"Yeah, Navajo on my mother's side."

"Okay, I'm gonna help you with the radios and whatever else. We got a couple guys in this platoon who are going to fuck with you, most likely. This ain't basic training or head games, it's real shit. Over here, you do what you gotta do and you'll be alright. When we go outside the wire and get out of the trucks, don't bunch up with anybody. Pay attention. Everybody outside the wire is a shithead. Damn near all of them, but that's close enough."

"That's fucked up."

"I know, but this platoon doesn't fuck around. We're part of an infantry company, we've been outside the wire a bunch of times already, and nobody is fucking with us. Why do you think that is? We got guys that are on their third tour over here, they know what's up. Pretty soon you'll see, there's guys in this platoon that don't fuck around. We got a big white boy from Oklahoma and a crazy Dominican from Philly. It's no joke over here. Until you got here, I was the newest guy in the platoon, and I been here almost a year."

"What the fuck?"

"Yeah, what the fuck. They used to smoke the dogshit out of me, but they won't do that too much over here because of the heat, and they don't want to fuck somebody up and take them outside the wire and you're useless, you know? You'll be up all night doing patrols, so get sleep whenever you can. It's fucked up out there, people getting fucked up but so far nobody has fucked with this platoon. The shitheads aren't happy with us. You'll feel it when you go out there. When you're back here, you eat and sleep and that's it.

Don't be fucking around with phone calls and all that shit. This place wears you down fast, but we got each other's back in this platoon. That's all that matters. Put your rifle back together and I'll show you some shit with the radios."

"Thanks, specialist," the private said as he started to reassemble his weapon. "Can I ask where you're from?"

"Yeah, you can ask. I'm from Texas."

8

The few weeks of early summer were hard for the platoon. For Joe, it started with watching the new private being introduced to the group. His name was Stillwater. He grew up near Twin Arrows, Arizona, and some of his ancestry was Native American on his mother's side of the family. The kid was tall and lanky, with dark hair and skin. Briggs messed with the kid right away, hiding his weapon and other items to confuse him. It was part of a process for Briggs, the same as he had gone through and had passed on to Joe when he was new.

The weeks that started in June and stretched into July were hard for everyone. They were on patrol when the platoon leader's truck was hit by an IED, their first enemy contact. The Humvee disappeared when it happened a little after ten o'clock in the morning, as the mounted patrol passed a vacant lot heaped upon with trash. Joe's mind went blank when he saw Lieutenant Redd's truck vanish, the echo of the blast went away, and in the moments that followed. He looked for the truck that was hit and saw nothing but dust and debris. The voice of the young officer crackled over the radio as he made his report to company headquarters.

"Baja X-Ray! Contact, IED!"

Joe dismounted the truck with a medic bag, dismounted his truck behind the stricken vehicle, and ran toward the damaged truck. A gunner atop one of the trucks shouted from behind his machine gun to stay put and pull security.

In the aftermath of the explosion, Iraqi civilians began to emerge from their houses and onto the street to watch. Joe pointed his rifle at every man, woman, and child he saw, his right thumb switching the selector lever of his rifle from safe to fire, his right index finger pressed against the trigger.

"Get the fuck out of here!" he yelled at them.

The civilians shrank back into their homes at Joe's show of force. The gunner yelled at him. "Hey Cuero, we gotta haul ass back to the FOB! We got casualties!"

Joe returned to his truck and the platoon sped back toward the base, the Humvees running numerous civilian vehicles off the road along the way. Radio chatter was non-stop, much of it indecipherable, as voices crackled and popped out of the speakers. Lieutenant Redd's voice was there intermittently; the platoon leader sounded fired up, but not frantic. Joe focused on his breathing while a feeling of optimism came upon him, listening to the officer as he received reports from different truck commanders, coalesced the data, and sent his reports up to the company commander, painting a picture of what was happening.

The convoy's full-tilt dash toward base abruptly stopped at a checkpoint manned by the Iraqi Army. The truck that had been hit by the IED had given out. Coolant and oil streamed from its motor and flowed onto the hot, asphalt road. The truck would not move any farther, yet it continued to idle as if it were a stubborn soldier, refusing to surrender.

The driver's door opened and a sergeant jumped out as the passenger door behind him opened. Briggs tumbled out of the truck and onto the ground, through the grasp of the sergeant trying to brace him. Briggs' head had been wrapped with an Israeli bandage. Blood covered his left side, from his head to his boots. A combat medic started working on an open wound to his neck.

Other soldiers joined the effort and helped Briggs to his feet. They put him into the truck commanded by Sergeant First Class Young. That truck and another Humvee raced away to finish the medical evacuation. The rest of the platoon pulled security at the checkpoint and waited for reinforcements from Baja Company to arrive and hook up a tow bar to the damaged vehicle. The recovery mission ended at JSS Medina, where the platoon learned that Briggs had been seriously injured.

The bomb was a 155mm artillery shell that had been rigged to a radio-controlled detonator. Briggs was lucky. A piece of shrapnel entered his forehead, traveled around his skull and exited through the back of his head. He was hit in the neck as well, with the shrapnel missing his carotid artery by a few inches. He was being readied for an emergency flight to Balad, Iraq, then to Maryland for additional medical treatment. After that, he would be released and return home to Oklahoma to spend time with his family. Lieutenant Redd immediately put in the paperwork for the Purple Heart award and the Combat Action Badge.

The clutter of conversations and agitated thoughts finally subsided, but Joe was confident he shared a similar feeling as the others, that the platoon reacted just as it had been trained when the moment of truth occurred. Putting aside his anger at the enemy's audacity, he could see how the actions of individuals and the group saved Briggs' life. Joe had seen enough in the preceding weeks to deal with the animosity growing within him toward the shitheads.

He resented the enemy to a certain degree, but as the platoon sergeant said, the enemy was just doing his job. Any ill temper Joe had for the shitheads was tolerated, like putting up with the constant smell of something that was burning, day or night, leaving an acrid taste in his mouth. It seemed always to be there, and so there was nothing to do about it. Payback would be a function, like gears meshing in a clock, passing time without emotion.

Troubled thoughts came and went through the rest of the day and into the night as Joe went off to sleep. The platoon was back together at JSS Medina, having reassembled when Briggs was taken to Camp Liberty. The excitement had died down and the normal routine returned. In the darkness, someone shook Joe out of a light sleep.

"Get ready to go," the voice said.

One of the infantry platoons had been hit by an IED. Dim lights flickered throughout the sleeping quarters and cast fluttering shadows on the walls as soldiers bustled about, grabbing gear that had been prearranged for a quick response. The platoon mounted its trucks and scrambled toward its objective. The radios buzzed with traffic. It was clear that something serious had gone down. A catastrophic kill in the middle of the night, with four dead and an understrength platoon trying to provide security until help arrived.

Joe drove one of the Humvees. He steered the truck around a corner, and they arrived at the scene of the attack. At an intersection just ahead, there was armored Humvee, upside down and engulfed in fire, by the side of the road. Joe pushed down on the brakes and Lieutenant Redd and others got out of the truck. At the platoon leader's instruction, Joe drove past the wreckage, the only other occupant of his vehicle being Fisher, who was manning the fifty-caliber machine gun in the turret. Joe eased the truck past the blast site. He saw pieces of charred arms and legs that littered the road and sidewalk. Joe pushed the accelerator and the vehicle bumped over body parts as he went. A sick feeling took hold of his stomach. Once past the kill zone, he stopped the truck at a four-way intersection, facing away from the destroyed Humvee.

He sat there for the next six hours without saying a word to Fisher. They listened to the radio in the darkness as the nightmare unfolded. Joe's mind foraged for something to break the monotony of staring through the windshield.

Two of the four bodies were not found for some time. An Iraqi woman led the search team to her back yard, about seventy-five meters from the explosion. She had covered the remains of one of the soldiers with a blanket. Body parts were gathered from farther away. Truck parts were brought out of people's yards. There were sensitive items that could not be found, such as weapons and night-vision equipment.

As dawn creeped over the eastern sky, Joe's platoon finished the recovery mission, left the area and made its way to Camp Liberty. He drove while thinking about the soldiers that had been killed. Death came for soldiers that had made an impression on everyone who knew them. The dead included Major Lawrence, the battalion's operations officer. Joe had met the major back at home station in Georgia. Major Lawrence made frequent visits to Joe's company, which was unusual for an operations officer.

Another soldier killed in the IED strike was the senior medic Staff Sergeant Gratton, who was on his fourth tour of duty in the Middle East after experiencing combat first as a light infantryman more than a decade earlier during Desert Storm. Gratton was as crusty and gruff as any infantryman in Baja Company, but he was first and foremost a lifesaver. He was short and squat of build, but his demeanor was in total contrast to his appearance. He often talked about what the Army termed "buddy aid," those critical moments when a soldier's training can keep another soldier alive until the next level of care can be received. Keeping another soldier alive, just for a few moments until a combat medic arrived, could be the difference between life and death, Doc Gratton often said. His words prior to their departure from Kuwait still wafted through Joe's mind at that moment.

Take care of each other.

Despite being the senior medic in the battalion, Gratton had volunteered to be the senior medic of Baja Company, because he knew the infantry company was sure to come under fire early and often during The Surge. Now he was gone.

Also taken were two soldiers Joe barely knew. One was a specialist from Guam, whose infantry brothers said came to their platoon out of shape, only able to perform eight sit-ups to the Army standard. But he soon remedied his lack of fitness and molded himself into a hardcore infantryman.

Another of the dead, a private first class, was the youngest soldier they lost that night. He was twenty years old and from New Jersey. When Joe crossed paths with the infantryman, they said hello and nothing else. The young soldier had already earned the respect of his older comrades when, during a brief firefight, he drove his Bradley Fighting Vehicle between a group of shitheads and an American soldier hit by small-arms fire. His actions provided cover and concealment for his buddies as they prepped the wounded soldier for medical evacuation. His quick thinking was well and beyond what some might have expected from a young soldier in the heat of battle, and then he was gone, going home.

The remains were taken to Camp Liberty, where the body bags were unloaded from the trucks by soldiers Joe had never seen before. No words were spoken to break the lull that hung in the morning air. Joe and Fisher were sent to a detail behind a wall of concrete barriers. Several metal barrels were filled with diesel fuel, as well as the uniforms and body armor that had been taken from the soldiers' bodies. A pile of drab-green ammunition cans was nearby, and Joe and Fisher were instructed to go through the cans and separate any sensitive items from them before the rest of the contents were burned.

They worked quietly and followed orders, putting aside pieces of night vision devices and weapons, broken and burned beyond use. They also made a pile of equipment such as sunglasses, carabiners, knives, and shemagh scarves. Everything was placed inside the fiery barrels. All the things the dead carried were burned, out of view of anyone, except for the two soldiers fulfilling the duty they were told to carry out. They stared blankly into the flames while the black smoke ascended into the morning sky.

In the aftermath, Baja Company regrouped and kept going. Joe attended a ceremony at an airfield as his brothers were placed on a transport plane to be taken back to their families. He listened to the chaplain pray for the souls of the soldiers as their flag-draped caskets were loaded onto the plane. It took the deaths of four soldiers for those in charge of running the war to authorize Joe's platoon to remount its tanks. The night following the catastrophic kill, the tank platoon began counter-IED patrols in Al-Jami'ah.

On a hot night in Baghdad a few days into the new routine, Joe was using a handheld spotlight to scan the road from his Abrams tank. He saw a blue wire running across a three-way intersection and along a curb. He was in the loader's position atop the tank, with Lieutenant Redd as the tank commander. Joe had taken the job left behind by Briggs. Joe and the platoon leader visually traced the wire, which ran behind their tank, over a wall, and into a house. Joe started to feel anger and frustration well up within him over the soldiers they had lost a few nights beforehand. It was payback time, like a clock ticking in his head.

Sergeant First Class Young's tank went to work first. It bashed through the concrete wall of the house, reducing it to rubble. He ordered his driver to run over a car that was parked in front of the house, flattening the vehicle within seconds. Some of the wreckage twisted into the left side of the tank's track, so Joe and Lieutenant Redd dismounted and tried to wrench free the metal from the platoon sergeant's fender and track. It was stuck, and Joe pulled security while other tankers dismounted their vehicles, grunted and pulled at the mangled steel, finally setting it free. The tankers remounted and set a perimeter around the block. The house wherein the blue wire vanished sat silent in the dark night. Set in the safety of his loader's hatch, Joe still felt a flush of anger within him. He tried to hold it down.

"Cuero, you've been begging me to throw one of these grenades for the longest time," Lieutenant Redd said. "You ready?"

In a flash, Joe had a grenade in his hand and his thumb on the safety clip.

"Let me get down first," the platoon leader said. "You know what you're doing."

Joe thumbed off the safety clip and pulled the pin. With the grenade in his right hand, he pointed his left arm toward the target house, reared back his right arm like a quarterback ready to throw, then launched the grenade in a line drive toward the house. He watched briefly as the grenade sailed over a row of bushes and clattered against a front window then, as trained, he dropped into the safety of the tank and yelled, "frag out!"

From within the tank, Joe heard the *whump* of the grenade exploding. He and the platoon leader popped up out of their tank to see a cloud of smoke near the impact area. The house started to catch fire, giving Joe a feeling of anticipation that washed over his mind.

Burn to the ground, motherfucker.

The fire quickly died, leaving the building intact. A handful of soldiers dismounted the tanks and searched the house. It was empty but they found IED-making materials such as bundles of wire and wire cutters. They found a gas mask in an upstairs bedroom. It did not come close to avenging the deaths of their infantry comrades, but at least they were picking up a scent along the trail.

Back in the relative safety of JSS Medina, Sergeant First Class Young conducted the after-action review.

"Anybody want to go home? You boys had enough?" he asked, a nonchalant look on his face, barely visible in the darkness. He lit a cigar and drew slowly, savoring the aromatic smoke.

"No, sarn't," several voices called out.

"That's good to hear. You guys were sensational tonight. Good job finding that IED. That's why we're here. Good work all the way around. Like you heard me say many times, tighten your shot group. Every day. You wanna add anything, sir?"

"Thanks, Sergeant Young," Elijah Redd said.

When the platoon sergeant walked away to enjoy his cigar, Elijah spoke. "That's the best platoon sergeant in the Army," he said.

"Hard core," one soldier said.

"Old school," another agreed. "You see him put his tank over that car and through the wall?"

Laughter went up through the platoon as the soldiers rejoiced in their victory. They had not captured anybody, but they located another IED before it detonated, leaving plenty of forensic evidence for EOD and military intelligence to sort through.

"Cuero got the oldest eyes in the platoon, but he saw that wire first!"

"Damn straight!"

Boisterous voices sounded off in unison.

"Cuero! Cuero! Cuero!"

"Alright, settle it down," Elijah said. "I'm going to tell you the same thing the platoon sergeant just said, but I think it bears repeating. You're good at this. This was a team win. Counter-IED measures work. You're proving it every day. But don't forget, the enemy learns from his mistakes, just like we learn from ours. He's going to adapt. He's going to come back and try again."

"Not in the house Cuero blew up with that grenade!"

Another round of laughter swept through the platoon. Soldiers slapped each other on the back. A few of them gathered around Joe, feigning punches into his midsection and patting him roughly on the head. For the first time in his life, he felt like he belonged.

"Alright, alright," Elijah said. "We're done here. Go get some sleep."

9

The Surge ramped up as July crawled along, one grueling day at a time. The platoon was briefed about the newest bad guy on the radar, a man for whom a "Be On the Look Out," or BOLO, had been issued. Criminal activity remained high in Baghdad despite efforts by American commanders to provide steadfast coverage over their assigned areas. IED attacks had become the enemy's standard procedure in the aftermath of the catastrophic hit against Baja Company. Day by day, junior officers received their orders, briefed their soldiers, and embarked on mounted and dismounted patrols in search of the enemy. The Americans became entrenched in a battle of wills against their adversaries as well as the unrelenting heat.

Lieutenant Elijah Redd had entertained the idea of joining the Mississippi Department of Wildlife, Fisheries and Parks when he was in high school. He hunted white-tailed deer on his family's property when he was a boy; spellbound by the natural world of the coastal plains near Hattiesburg where he went to Southern Miss and earned his bachelor's degree in criminal justice.

He joined the Reserve Officer Training Corps (ROTC) in his freshman year in college because he was good with a rifle and he wanted something to do while at school besides overwhelming himself in academics. The discipline of military life was like second nature to him. He took elective courses in philosophy and discovered *Nausea* by Jean-Paul Sartre, feeling a tingling of unrest as he flipped through the pages. Rather than go to law school at Ole Miss, he accepted an officer's commission in the Army.

He sensed the frustration growing within his platoon. His soldiers were going about the tedious routine of patrols and keeping an eye out for several people of interest. The platoon set its trucks in an outer cordon to establish security for an infantry platoon going from one house to the next, clearing buildings and looking for signs of enemy activity. The newest shithead on their list of targets was like many of the others, with a name as indecipherable to Elijah and his men as a bowl of alphabet soup.

The jitters had worn off, and they came to know the reality of their situation a few weeks into the deployment. Between Briggs getting hit and the IED strike that killed four soldiers and seriously injured another that night in June, the platoon needed just an atomic particle of luck, the lieutenant surmised.

Out of nowhere, the moment arrived. The suspect was caught and identified during a cordon-and-search mission. He was seen at a nearby mechanic's shop a few days earlier, but he got into a taxi and avoided capture by a swarm of trucks and tanks that had given chase. Once the man was captured and his identity was confirmed, a wave of exuberance swept through the platoon, as news of the victory sounded from the radios in their trucks.

Once they had their man in custody, the soldiers were told by Iraqi police on the spot that he worked as an asset for the Iraqi Army and was released. The subject of their good fortune disappeared, receding into the city. Back at JSS Medina, the first floor of the tank platoon's living quarters offered a place to unwind from the mission. Soldiers peeled off their body armor and laid down on their beds.

A cacophony of music, cursing and laughter bounced from the musty walls of the building as the soldiers came down from the rush of the hunt. Every time they went out, their return included a brief meeting to discuss what they learned from the mission.

Soldiers spent the rest of their free time within the confines of the old schoolhouse. Its walls reverberated with sounds of music and conversation, and weapons being disassembled for cleaning and inspection. Equipment was unpacked and packed again for the next mission.

Joe checked his survival equipment, one item at a time.

Weapon, combat lifesaver bag, night vision, water, map...

Mindful of a briefing from the Army's Asymmetric Warfare Group he attended at home station in Georgia, he holstered his pistol with clips of ammunition to his belt. In extreme circumstances, he could shed most of his gear in a matter of seconds while retaining the most essential items for survival. He studied *Warfighting Handbook*, which was published by the 3rd Infantry Division for the deployment. The handbook defined an IED as "the end product of a complex set of enemy activities."

Sitting on his cot and cleaning his rifle, Joe tried to block the images in his mind. He tried to think of his experiences when he was a boy, watching Dick Clark on television each New Year's Eve, with his parents off to some party and his grandmother getting drunk on Seagram's whiskey and soda while babysitting Joe and his brothers and sisters. Or the winter nights in Texas when the family home's only heat came from the kitchen stove. Now he was almost forty years old and looking for the devil himself, it seemed, in the streets of Baghdad.

When it ventured into the city, the platoon was either on foot or on mounted patrol in its Humvees. The soldiers' diet was mostly dehydrated food. Occasionally, some of the more adventurous would eat food from the local markets. Most of the time they ate falafel, typically made up of chickpeas, herbs, and goat meat, but Joe did not venture into the local cuisine.

This was not combat with gunfights and attack helicopters. It was drive-by shootings with AK-47s, *pop-pop-pop* and the shitheads were gone. In the aftermath, a soldier would be on the ground, blood streaming out of him and his buddies scrambling to patch him up and get him back to the FOB. Soldiers were getting shot or blown apart, nearly as a daily occurrence. There were some he knew and there were others who were a familiar name and nothing else. There were some he never knew at all, but it did not make much difference.

It took the catastrophic killing of their fellow soldiers for Joe's platoon to be returned to their tanks. There was a growing frustration over the enemy's ability to set the terms of the fight. On a clear summer night while on patrol, the platoon came upon a car that seemed out of place.

Decisions were made in the haste of time evaporating. They were looking for another BOLO individual in the area, and the car matched the description of a vehicle he was said to be using for the employment of IEDs. It was about fifty meters down the street, parked by a curb in front of what looked like an abandoned house.

The BOLO was known only as the Fat Man. EOD came out, set a charge in the trunk and blew the car to smithereens, shattering the night with amber sparks and a billow of smoke.

Moments later, Joe's tank crew opened fire with its machine guns. Tracer rounds bounced off the car and skipped across the road, ricocheting into the evening sky before burning out. There was no secondary explosion, Joe observed while he watched from the safety of his tank's hatch, and the white sedan smoldered in fire, casting shadows on nearby buildings.

Using personal night-vision devices, Joe and others from his tank could see a group of what appeared to be military-aged men emerging from the darkness of the street. They wore dishdashas and milled about the destroyed vehicle before making their way toward the tanks. Joe feathered the trigger of his machine gun as they approached.

Get ready to die, shitheads.

The men, about six that Joe could see, carried AK-47s and would soon be meeting their God. There was a burst of radio traffic from another tank crew. It was the voice of Staff Sergeant Badger. "Dismounts, no tape!"

The absence of Infrared Tape (IR) tape on the men suggested they were, indeed, enemy combatants, as all coalition forces wore the IR or "glint" tape to identify them as friendlies. Joe nestled into a solid position behind his machine gun and readied himself to pull the trigger. In warning, the radio crackled again.

"Friendlies possible! Wait one!"

Joe watched from his loader's station as Badger dismounted his tank and approached the men on foot. Badger, barely visible in the dark, remounted his vehicle. The radio came alive again with his report.

"Friendly forces times thirty-two, and they're pissed off."

Joe's tank platoon had stumbled across a Special Forces unit, dressed like the locals, doing who knew what, looking to grab hold of Satan's tail. The tank platoon's mission was aborted, subjugated under that of the Green Berets on the ground, who asserted they had cleared their mission under the command of the organization Joe's platoon had replaced weeks earlier.

The Green Berets may not have known how close they were to getting ripped apart by machine-gun fire, but the tank platoon's mission was dropped, and they returned to Camp Liberty for a debriefing. They listened to music over the vehicle's radio system as they made their way back to base. Bad Religion blared in his brain as he watched the buildings pass by, and shards of red and green tracer fire streaked through the sky like shooting stars.

Once at Camp Liberty, the tank platoon dismounted and stowed its equipment back at the sleep tent. Joe wilted into the comfort of his cot as the hum of music echoed through the tent. He lowered the volume on his laptop computer and dozed off.

Joe sat upright in his bed out of a deep sleep. The world was dark and quiet inside the tent. People were talking outside. Joe could make out the voices of Fisher and Sergeant First Class Young. Joe heard Fisher complaining about something. Fisher was not one to kick up a fuss, having been through two deployments already. Joe leaned forward, trying to make something out of the distant conversation.

"All we're doing is driving around waiting to get fucked up," Fisher said, "setting off IEDs with our thumbs up our own ass the whole time. Don't make no sense to me watching dudes get fucked up for nothing. These dudes have families. What the fuck are we doing? This shit feels like the end of the road when I have to look at these guys every day and think, what the fuck is happening?"

"This time around got you all twisted," Young said, his voice sounding dull and far away. "It's like a girl you know and she ain't right for you, but you with her anyway. You can see it in her eyes, there ain't nothing there. It's all uphill. Then one day she's gone. You surprised? No, cause it's over. You pick up the pieces and go. You've been waiting for it, and it's here, and you go on your way. But when she was still around and you were going through the motions, that fucked up feeling stays with you even after she leaves. That's what the fuck is up right here."

"And that's it?" Fisher asked.

"Naw, you just keep going and don't think too much."

Fisher was a North Philly guy, and the platoon sergeant was a stubborn, by-the-book lifer from Georgia. Joe was curious as to how many of these conversations happened between them over the years. He felt a pinch of guilt about it, eavesdropping on a debate between soldiers with more experience in combat than he would likely ever know. He lowered the volume of his laptop another notch to hear the conversation.

"I was made for this shit," Fisher said. "My dad wasn't around much. My uncles were locked up in Graterford and Eastern State. My grandad, too. But if one of them caught me doing any ill shit they would whip my ass with a belt. They wanted me to stay straight and get out of Philly. They had a party for me before I went to boot camp. They didn't have no idea what the fuck was about to happen to me, that's what I was thinking at the time. But now I look at it and think, maybe they did."

The next day, Joe sat down with the new kid, Stillwater, to show him a few things. They were on the roof of JSS Medina, around noon, sitting in one of the bunkers and pulling security in case the enemy tried to attack the building. Joe held an operator's manual for the Monocular Night Vision Device (MNVD), which was standard Army issue.

"Look, new guy. What the fuck were you listening to on your laptop, Merle Haggard? Never mind, it doesn't matter. Check this out. You get into a firefight or separated from the platoon, you need to know how to use this shit," Joe said, leafing through the pages of the operator's manual. "This isn't a video game, okay?"

Stillwater looked at him, nodded as if he understood, and Joe continued.

"I got separated from the platoon one time on a foot patrol," Joe said. "Just like that. We were clearing a house, and I went to take a shit for ten minutes. When I came out, everybody was gone. Just like that."

"Are you serious?"

"Yeah, just like that. I went outside the house and they were gone. It was daylight and I knew their direction of travel, so when I ran down the street and around the corner, there they were. I thought I was about to end up on CNN getting my head cut off. The shit out here can turn bad so fast that you won't believe it. Imagine if I didn't find them and had to spend the night in that house by myself, waiting for someone to come looking for me? You need to know your equipment, so let's get into this."

The young soldier appeared to be eager to learn, as far as Joe could tell. Private Stillwater was going to have to figure things out quickly. Just then, Badger walked up.

"What the fuck are you doing?" he demanded.

"Showing Stillwater how the NVDs work," Joe replied.

"You're supposed to be pulling security, not giving a fucking class. Watch your sector, and after the shift is over, both of you come see me."

"Roger, staff sergeant."

10

Briggs sat in a metal folding chair among a group of soldiers arranged in a semi-circle around a slightly built woman who led a discussion on PTSD. The group session was mandatory, otherwise Briggs would have gone fishing that day. Inside the room, its beige-colored walls bare except for a blank, dry erase board, the woman called upon a young, clean-cut looking Hispanic man dressed in fatigues to "share" what happened to him the previous weekend.

"On Friday, everybody was gone so I went straight home," he said, slumped in his chair and looking down at the floor with his arms crossed over his chest. "Didn't even get undressed and out of uniform. I went by the dog park on the way home and saw a bunch of people were there. I got home and threw David in the truck and went over there. That's my dog's name, David Houston."

"Your dog's name is David Houston?" the woman said.

"That's right," he said. "Anyhow, I usually take him there later in the day, when there's just a few dogs and it's dark because the lights there bother me for some reason. So, there's a whole field of dogs there and he was hyper. Running to one couple and their dog, then to this dog, playing over there. This person here and that person there. I was running around just trying to keep him from jumping on people. He's just a puppy and he's excited, so I let him play for about thirty minutes before I got tired of chasing him. I put him in the truck and went home. I did a full, thorough cleaning of the apartment, top to bottom, everything. Gave David a bath, cleaned his kennel. The weekend went by fast. I didn't sleep much. I'm used to sleeping in, but my sleep schedule is off. I've been waking up and thinking. I'll do some laundry for next week and end up cleaning the room, then cleaning the whole apartment. Then it's two o'clock in the morning and I'm wide awake. I'm thinking I should probably sleep, but I can't. No nightmares or anything, but when I do fall asleep, I can't stay asleep and I get about two hours max, then I get up. I go to P.T. and after that I go to my truck and pass out."

Briggs slouched in his chair and waited for another round of sharing. Same empty walls, with most of the soldiers sitting around him either busted for doing drugs or so-called, "psych cases."

A soldier with what sounded like a German accent started talking. He was older than the others, his uniform and boots faded. Briggs had an urge to excuse himself from the group, go outside to his truck in the parking lot and get a slug of whiskey from the bottle hidden under the seat.

"Nothing spectacular this weekend," the man said. "I just sat around at the house, watched a few movies. Went to pick my daughter on Friday around noon, in Denton. Didn't do much Saturday. Just watched a little television. Talked to my wife and daughter a little bit. Pretty much lounged around. On Sunday I started on my homework, tried to finish it up. I looked at something and started to think about that cognitive… whatever it was."

"Distortion," Briggs said, wondering why the words from his mouth betrayed the disdain he had for everyone in the room. Again, there was the Hispanic woman, Puerto Rican he guessed by her accent, taking notes and overseeing the conversation.

"Right. Cognitive distortion. Because I'm always right. Not really, but you know, whatever. I caught myself doing that again. As I did that, I caught myself and told myself, "I'll try." I tried. It's hard. Then I tried to read another chapter, and I caught myself drifting, thinking about work and people pissing me off about something. I was all over the place. And that was about it. I really didn't do too much."

"Any difficulties or problems?" the woman asked.

"No, just thinking about some things this week. Some appointments and finishing up with the V.A. Small stuff."

The woman shifted in her chair and looked at another soldier. A soldier that looked like he was older than most. His hair and skin were dark, probably a Hispanic. His eyes found Briggs, and he started talking.

"I was born in Huntington Beach, California, not because I was a rich Hollywood movie star. In fact, it was about an hour's drive to the Walk of Fame from where I grew up. My dad was in the Navy, and we were stationed at the Naval Weapons Station at Seal Beach when I was born. Lived there a while and bounced around some coastal areas. We settled in Galveston, Texas, when he finally retired. My dad was an alcoholic. Drinking every day was part of life in our house, and I just thought it was normal."

The soldier paused, looking down at his weathered hands. He seemed lost in his thoughts for several moments, then continued.

"Back in the day when I was a private, our drill sergeants loved to play those mind games. They would catch us in the laundry room sleeping, then lay down on a machine and go to sleep. We were like, what the fuck is going on? They would say, "this is how stupid it looks when you guys do stupid shit," and then they would tell us, "everybody on the ready line," and we were like, "fuck, it's about to get stupid." Right before we would get smoked for hours, they would say, "privates, we know you get tired, we know you want to sleep sometimes, but this is what it looks like to the enemy, and you don't get much sleep because we always fuck with you because you're stupid as fuck, but, do the right thing at the right time," and we would say, "yes drill sergeant," and after two hours of getting smoked, we were done. Then they would say, "alright, privates, we're done. Now go back to bed," and all we could say was, "alright, drill sergeant."

Briggs looked around the room. Every time somebody talked, the others just looked at the floor, nodding their heads, whether out of indifference or because they understood every word being said. Briggs couldn't tell. Another soldier, a female officer, seemingly in her early fifties but without any rank insignia on her chest, chimed in on the conversation.

"It's been said that genetics loads the gun and environment pulls the trigger, and I definitely believe that happened with me," she said. She leaned forward, staring at Briggs, making him so uncomfortable that he looked away.

"I'm not sure I'm in the right group," Briggs said, shifting his immense body in the chair and looking at the Puerto Rican woman in charge of the group. She scribbled something on a notepad in her lap and did not acknowledge his protest.

The older, female soldier continued with her story. "I first drank at the age of thirteen in 1980, on the way to some concert in Houston," she said. "Somebody had the ability to buy beer, so we're drinking beer in this guy's pickup truck. It wasn't anything fancy. It might have been Schlitz Malt Liquor or Pabst Blue Ribbon. I just remember this nasty taste, and I almost had to throw up, but I was able to keep it down and then the feeling hit me, and I liked it. I was about to go into high school, and so drinking became part of my high school environment. My criteria for high school was to pick an extracurricular activity that got me out of class the most because I didn't like school. It wasn't that I was a bad student. I got good grades. I just didn't like it. I was restless, irritable, and discontented. I was bored in the classroom, and I just wanted to get away from it. It turned out it was the rifle team that traveled the most, and so I decided I was going to join. To be on the rifle team, I had to join the junior ROTC, so I did. We marched around the quad, did stuff like that. It was my rifle coach that talked me into applying to West Point, so that's how I ended up in the Army."

Briggs was relieved when the Puerto Rican woman's watch started beeping. It was a signal for the group to take a break. He wasn't sure what he was doing in that classroom, with a group of soldiers talking like people he listened to while attending Alcoholics Anonymous meetings with his father when he was a boy. His dad wasn't around much between working the oil rigs in West Texas, stretches in jail, and being vacant even when he was at home, drunk or high on drugs.

Just as he experienced when he was growing up, Briggs was again listening to people talk aimlessly about drugs and booze with no end in sight to their ramblings. What did that have to do with him, he wondered. He was on convalescent leave in Oklahoma, attending mandatory sessions about combat stress at Fort Sill, waiting to heal from his wounds so that he could rejoin his platoon in Iraq. That was all that mattered to Briggs. The Army doctors diagnosed him with Post-Traumatic Stress Syndrome, ordered him to attend group counseling while his shrapnel wounds healed, and advised him to get ready for life outside the military.

As far as Briggs was concerned, the doctors could go fuck themselves. Between the group sessions, he would go out to his pickup truck, an old Chevy his grandfather had left him when he died. Briggs would sip whiskey and listen to old Patti LaBelle & The Bluebells songs on the truck's 8-track tape player. There was a massacre going on all over the world. His rightful place as a soldier was with his buddies. As much as he felt that road held nothing but a dead end, every day back in the states was more strain than he could bear.

11

Captain Zach Davis watched an illumination round go skyward into a somber August night. He sat in a chair on the rooftop of Medina and read after-action reports from recent missions conducted by his soldiers. The tempo of combat operations in their sector was astonishing. Enemy activity spiked as soon as Baja Company arrived and went outside the wire in early June.

In between missions and within the relative safety of the Medina compound, the soldiers either provided security in the guard towers or they slept. There was no time for anything else. The shitheads were always looking for an opportunity to attack; a lesson Zach had learned when he was a new lieutenant a few years earlier. The battlespace had changed since his first taste of action. As an infantry commander, his job was to guide his soldiers along a path with tactical patience on one side of the road and violence of action on the other.

He grew up in a small town just west of California's San Fernando Valley and played quarterback in high school. Among his heroes while in high school was Mark Brunell, a highly regarded quarterback from just up the coast and a few years older than Zach, who wanted to follow in his idol's footsteps to the University of Washington. Instead, Zach went to Fresno State.

He tried to make the football team as a walk on his freshman year but didn't make it. He selected history for a major and along the way developed an interest in the school's military science program, which led him to enter Army service as a commissioned officer. His studies in high school awakened within him an interest in the history of the western frontier, which once covered North Dakota to Texas. He was enthralled by the Army's campaigns during the Indian wars and the push into the new frontier. He searched beyond the classroom for knowledge and read everything Francis Paul Prucha wrote that Zach could find. Deep within the caldron of academics and military training, his experience sharpened his appetite for American history in the early Nineteenth Century.

The War of 1812 gave American soldiers a rite of passage defending their home. Many who experienced the muck and sorrow of war carried those lessons into the Indian campaigns and the war with Mexico, and Zach was absorbed in the history of those experiences.

After years of college and military training, he cut his teeth as a lieutenant during the invasion in 2003. It was a "weapons free" environment, which meant soldiers could engage suspected enemy targets at will. Errors in judgement sometimes cost innocent people their lives. Being in combat was like watching a fire, its embers sparking from time to time, and then the light went away, and feeling the place cold and dark again.

Zach leaned against a concrete wall on the roof of the Medina compound and looked up at the night sky. The same stars from the night before were out. As a company commander, Zach was tasked with finding allies in the makeshift Iraqi government with which to partner. If the Army hadn't made such a big deal about delving into the hearts and minds of the local population, Zach could have unleashed the tank platoon attached to his company and be done with it all.

A soldier's voice punctuated the darkness of Zach's thoughts. "Hey private, drop and start doing push-ups."

"What for?"

"You wanna know what for, private? Alright, get up, then. Who's the sergeant of the guard on duty?"

A burly infantryman stood outside one of the bunkers. In the dim haze of the night, Zach could make out another figure, a slender private being interrogated by the older infantryman. The sergeant often checked on the security guards standing watch on the rooftop.

"I will fuck you up, boy," the sergeant said. "You're up here standing watch with a fucking laptop computer, watching a movie? Grab your gear and get the fuck out of here. Go watch your fucking movie. You tankers are hot garbage. I got a replacement on the way up here for your sorry ass."

Zach watched as the young soldier that was admonished walked past him. Zach looked over the private as he passed by, observing his body language for anything signifying a lesson learned, having endangered the lives of his fellow soldiers that were downstairs, resting between patrols. But the commander could not make out anything in the darkness.

"Perdido," Zach said, exploring the moment for something meaningful, as if the private could grasp the severity of the situation. The security lapse was almost beyond the grasp of a logical mind. An Army sentry's first general order, "I will guard everything within the limits of my post, and quit my post only when properly relieved," was among the most solemn duties any soldier could undertake. And this youngster was watching a movie on a laptop computer. It was beyond annoying.

"Keep walking, shitbag," Zach snarled at the private as he walked past.

Zach rose from his chair. A soldier emerged from the stairway door and walked quietly to the guard post that had been vacated. The soldier was one of Zach's best. The replacement quietly brushed past the sergeant that had discovered the security breach and tunneled his way into the bunker to assume his watch behind a machine gun.

Zach had no reason to intervene. The commander returned his gaze toward the evening sky. Each time somebody fucked up, the shitheads were surely watching. He would not be able to talk to his wife about nights like this. Every mistake invited a catastrophic outcome. When his soldiers were blown apart by IEDs or hit by enemy snipers, he had a feeling of being alone, grasping at the aftermath. As the smoke drifted away, it left him in a miserable state of mind. Nothing left but to fill out paperwork, feeling dead tired and empty. The fight in Iraq was already dredging away at him. Just a few years ago, it was firefights and tales of valor on the part of the Americans. Gunfights like those from the American frontier in the books he devoured in his youth, foolish in his philosophies about the merits of being tested through combat.

How he wanted to let loose the tanks. Ballistic shielding, closed hatches, weapons blazing death across the city, as he had himself witnessed during the invasion. A commander's orders were to send out his soldiers like bait, then wait for the enemy to strike. Zach's soldiers did so with audacity. They set out on foot across the Field of Death and took fire, and some of his soldiers were hit. Some were carried in metal coffins to planes for the ride back home. Some of the lucky ones made it out on foot.

There were no laws in this place. It was only the crud and heat of the day, and then night fell to afford his soldiers, those magnificent grunts under his command, an advantage over the enemy. Superior technology and training against a faceless adversary. A quandary playing out in real time, trying to fix the enemy's location and destroy him. Sort of like playing cards with the angel of death, putting up the lives of his soldiers like chips on the table.

Zach was apprehensive in his thoughts. This was no time to be inattentive to opportunity. His job was to keep his men ready for that moment. Until then, it was going to be foot patrols. Knocking on doors and, in some cases, kicking them down. Zach could not pacify himself nor discern anything through the migraine headache that appeared suddenly as it had many times beforehand. It was a distinctive reminder that he needed to get some sleep. He made his way down the stairs and into the company's command post. A few soldiers were on duty, monitoring radio traffic.

He felt a mood of distress in the air. His company had discovered a few weapons caches during their initial push into its area of responsibility, but it was certain that the enemy had inflicted far more damage on the Americans. If there were a place somewhere in which his troops could turn the tide, it had yet to be found. As uneasy as Zach was over the situation, he had to get some sleep. He wanted more than anything to see his soldiers post a banner of victory in the streets of Baghdad, but it did not appear likely to happen that night while he laid down on his bunk. As he nodded off, he brought peace to his mind with Psalm 127:

> It is vain for you to rise up early, to sit up late,
> to eat the bread of sorrows: for so He giveth his beloved sleep.

12

Stillwater was late again. He was the last one to show up for another mission briefing, drawing unapproving stares from soldiers that fixed their eyes on him. The new guy had a personality that was too laid back to satisfy the expectations of more seasoned soldiers. The tank platoon was much smaller than the infantry platoons of Baja Company. As the tankers were continually reminded by the grunts, they were unversed in the doctrine of infantry tactics.

The tankers went on foot patrols in Baghdad daily. There were occasional tank patrols, which were intended to root out IEDs and project American firepower within sector. The tankers had several seasoned fighters from previous combat tours in Iraq. Everybody leaned on the wisdom of the more experienced soldiers. The goal of the platoon was to make itself a challenging target, one the enemy would have to be desperate to attack.

The standards for performance in the Army were simple. As most young soldiers were often told, if one showed up at the right time, at the right place, and wearing the correct uniform, success is all but guaranteed. Stillwater could not even get that right. Whether he was even trying was a matter of doubt within the platoon's leadership. The briefing had not begun, but roll call had already been taken, and he was not present when his name was called. A handful of his fellow privates were in a group, joking and smoking cigarettes, oblivious to his latest calamity.

"In basic, we had a guy who got his parents to sneak him a bottle of gin the mail, you know?" one of the privates said, relaying a story from boot camp. "God, that was a shit show for us when the drill sergeants found it."

Another private burst out, "Bro, who the fuck has parents like that? You got smoked for it?"

"Man, we got fucked up for that. One of the drill sergeants was like, "Privates, you know how much trouble you can get into for that? It's a criminal offense under the Uniform Code of Military Justice." And he was sipping on the bottle while he was ripping into us, and we were getting the dogshit smoked out of us."

The private punctuated his tale, which was likely somewhere between an embellished half-truth and a blatant lie, but his young comrades burst into laughter and exclamations of "aw, shit!" and "no fucking way!"

Joe listened to the story, which sounded like so many of the myths he had heard about basic training, as Stillwater eased up next to him. "Sorry I'm late, specialist. Had to take a shit."

Joe grunted his displeasure at the kid's excuse. In the absence of the injured Briggs, Joe was assigned the task of looking out for the fledgling. As one of the elders of the platoon, Joe had quickly earned a reputation as a door kicker, eager to be the first man into a room during search and clear missions. He was often chided by the higher ranking, more experienced soldiers much younger than he, many of them intent on taking him down a peg or two. He also suffered the banter of the youngest soldiers, mostly about his age but also his tastes in music and movies.

Meanwhile, Joe had proved himself adept at detecting even the most subtle of IED indicators. After seeing Briggs nearly killed by an improvised bomb, Joe had sworn to dedicate himself to the concept of IED defeat. Once he came to understand the IED as the end-product of enemy action, rather than merely an event, something turned for him. He could not be sure exactly what.

There would always be factors beyond his control. Namely, the financing, building, planning, and emplacing of bombs. Those activities were out of his lane, so Joe turned his attention on learning everything he could about the explosives, power sources, containers, and initiation devices that were being employed. He could see and touch those items, as they were found in weapons caches the platoons stumbled upon during routine patrols, or in the aftermath of IED attacks. The enemy was ever adapting, but Joe believed it possible to find traces of the bombs before they detonated. And he was proving his theory correct.

With Briggs back home, Joe inherited the job of looking after most of the privates. He eschewed the heavy handedness of Briggs for a more subtle approach, and he would deal with Stillwater's tardiness later, after the mission had ended.

The platoon went for a patrol in its Humvees and dismounted on a residential street. Soldiers got out of their trucks and quickly formed two files, with each column of soldiers occupying a sidewalk and advancing along the street. Within minutes, they made enemy contact. A sound that wrenched Joe's guts pierced the quiet of the daylit street.

Zzzzzzzzzzzzzzz

"Incoming!" a voice bellowed.

Zzzzzzzewwwww …. thunk!

Joe was face down beneath the rear end of a car, his hands covering his head. He waited a moment. "All clear!" a voice called out.

"What the fuck?" another's voice asked.

Joe looked up. A handful of soldiers had gathered next to a black, iron gate in front of a house. They looked down at a mortar round that had zipped down from the sky and hit the gate but did not explode.

"It's a dud!"

Gathered around the unexploded mortar, soldiers began pulling cameras from their pockets and snapping photos. The dirty air smelled the same as always. The street was quiet, void of civilian presence. Joe got to his feet. He held his rifle at the position of high ready and scanned about the nearby buildings, looking for anybody watching them while his fellow soldiers were snapping photographs. The rooftops and windows were as empty as the street. He kept his distance from the group that assembled near the mortar round. No sense in giving the enemy a target of opportunity by joining the crowd.

Joe lowered to one knee and lit a cigarette. He tried to control his breathing. The gut reaction was to relax in such a moment, and so he resisted, kept himself clear as he sensed his arms and legs, drenched in sweat, feeling heavy. Time kept going, and it became apparent it was not going to be a complex attack. The zing of the adrenaline rush ebbed away. He dropped the cigarette butt on the street and let the last of the smoke float out his mouth.

The big scene was all but over until an elderly man came out of a house and approached the commotion surrounding the mortar round. Lieutenant Redd and the platoon's interpreter, a Shiite they called Tony, talked to the civilian. After a brief conversation, word was passed that an IED had been emplaced ahead on the street, and the dud mortar that clanged harmlessly nearby may have spared the foot patrol from wandering into its kill zone.

Explosive Ordnance Disposal was summoned. The slow, deliberate pace of EOD operations closed the window of opportunity for the platoon to achieve its mission. Lieutenant Redd came up with an alternate course of action. He and the platoon sergeant led the dismounted soldiers from house to house, questioning civilians about enemy activity while drivers and gunners pulled security in the trucks, which blocked the street about three-hundred meters from the suspected IED.

The foot soldiers went to the home of the man who pointed out the danger. It was just the old man and his wife, who gave the soldiers chai tea in white, porcelain cups. They sipped the freshly brewed tea as Lieutenant Redd, with help from Tony, talked with the man. Joe leaned back in a chair in the kitchen, enjoying the tea. A group of sergeants passed the time discussing Hollywood starlets from the nineteen-seventies who aged gracefully, thirty years later. Brooke Shields and Farrah Fawcett were the co-champions of that category, the sergeants agreed.

One of the handheld radios announced the arrival of the company commander. A few moments later, Captain Davis entered the home. "What's new, Eli?" the commander asked, greeting the lieutenant with a hearty slap on the shoulder.

"Working on some intel, sir. This man saved us from having a bad day."

"I heard. I brought some money for him. Your guys are doing a good job out here," the commander said.

"Yes sir, they've been working hard."

The lieutenant turned his attention to the old man. He spoke directly to him as Tony interpreted, offering American cash for his help. It was five hundred dollars. The man waved his hands at the money in protest. Through the interpreter, he declined the reward.

"He said to keep your money," Tony said. "He says he wants to keep the area safe for the people who live here, and for the coalition forces that are here to help."

After more than a half-hour visiting the elderly couple, the Americans thanked them for their hospitality and moved on to another house. The momentum they felt as they departed was worn away by the remainder of their mission. At each place they went, the locals either claimed to have no knowledge of insurgents in the area, or they protested about the corruption within the Iraqi Army and police. Captain Davis stayed with the platoon to observe how the tankers acquitted themselves to the conduct of an infantry platoon on patrol.

Meanwhile, EOD discovered the suspected IED was an American illumination round that landed, nose down, in a vacant lot.

The round was a dud, its tailfins jutting out of the ground. EOD blew it up anyway. After three-and-a-half hours going from one house to the next, Lieutenant Redd ordered the men to remount the trucks. The temperature was well above one hundred degrees. On their way back to Medina, they came across a small group of Iraqi Army soldiers. One of them was laid out on his back, having succumbed to the heat.

The gunner for the platoon leader's Humvee grabbed several bottles of cold water from an ice chest in the truck and tossed them to the wilted soldier's comrades. The Americans were dumbstruck as the soldiers smiled and waved their arms in thanks. Instead of tending to their fallen comrade, they quickly uncapped the bottles of water and guzzled down the contents.

"Goddammit!" the gunner screamed. "They're chugging the water with their buddy laying there about to die, sir! What the fuck!"

"This is some of the dumbest shit I've ever seen," said the lieutenant. "I want to believe this country has a chance, but with these fuckers in charge, I'm not so sure."

Sitting behind the platoon leader, Joe shared the officer's opinion. "Nothing really makes you want to pack up and go home like that shit, eh sir? If we leave now, you can be home in time to catch the entire Southern Miss football season. Who do they start the year with?"

"Tennessee Martin," Elijah said. He had moved Joe to his crew after Briggs was injured and sent home. As the platoon leader, Elijah appreciated having Specialist Cuero around. While not nearly as experienced as Briggs, Joe Cuero had turned out to be as reliable as a hound dog when it came to sniffing out IEDs. Having seen what their first encounter with an improvised bomb did to Briggs, Elijah was eager to watch Joe firsthand.

"Your quarterback is Jeremy Young, right, sir?"

"Stop kissing the L.T.'s ass, Manny," said Fisher, sitting next to Joe in the back of the truck. "Southern Miss ain't shit."

"You're gonna be walking home, Fisher," Elijah said.

"Go ahead, sir. Let me out right here. This place ain't no worse than North Philly."

The lieutenant turned his attention back toward Joe. "We got a senior quarterback coming back, but it's gonna be tough to improve on winning nine games like we did last year."

"The young running back is the real deal," Joe said.

"Hell yeah. Damien Fletcher. He played high school ball in Biloxi, I believe it was."

Fisher pepped up again.

"Naw, Manny. Tyrone Wheatley, Michigan. That's a badass running back right there!"

"Listen, dumbass," Joe replied, "Ty Wheatley hasn't played college football for ten fucking years. If you wanna make a nuisance of yourself, at least know what the fuck you're talking about."

Outside the truck whirred the streets of Al-Jami'ah. Among the most effective counter-IED tactics for the Americans was moving as fast as their vehicles could manage. Mounted patrols resembled car chases from the movies, running civilian vehicles off the road and sending pedestrians scurrying to safety.

The Surge had ignited a spike in enemy activity against American and coalition forces across Iraq, especially Baghdad, where the culture minister himself was the subject of an arrest warrant. In the southwestern area of the city, a Sunni sheik had been assassinated in a drive-by shooting. Elsewhere in Baghdad, a gathering of tribal sheiks at a hotel was targeted by a suicide bomber. All hell was breaking loose across the capital, it seemed.

At JSS Medina, the platoon downloaded its gear and the soldiers returned to the sleeping area. Privates were ordered to report to Staff Sergeant Badger, who was waiting outside by the Humvees. They assembled in formation and stood at the position of attention, each soldier stiff as a board, awaiting the inevitable.

"Private Stillwater, front and center," Badger said.

"Roger. Moving, staff sergeant."

Stillwater stood before the staff sergeant, face to face.

"Private Stillwater, you're dismissed," Badger said, seething the words through clenched teeth. Stillwater did as he was told and hurried back into the building.

"What a nice day, huh? Wanna guess why we're out here?"

"Because Stillwater was late for the mission," one of the privates said.

"Close, but no cigar. Because you all failed him, that's why we're out here," Badger explained. "You see, privates, I don't have time for this shit. But you, I don't fucking get it. You refuse to pick up your battle buddy. Stillwater is new. Maybe that's it. Maybe it's because he's Native American, and you're a bunch of fucking racist motherfuckers, I don't know. Anyway, we're going to fix this, right here and now. Front-leaning rest position, move!"

The "front-leaning rest" was the push-up position.

Each soldier followed the order. For the next three hours, they were pushed through a journey of pain in the form of a series of punitive exercises known as a "smoke session," because Stillwater's failure to be on time for the most recent mission was deemed to be a failure on the part of the group, not the individual soldier. Stillwater's fellow privates languished through the session, several of them collapsing in the midday heat. The more they faltered, the more Badger poured it on. When it was over, everyone retreated to the sleeping area within the building.

Joe watched the privates trudge into their sleeping areas. He got up and peered behind a sheet that shielded Fisher's personal living space from view. Inside, Fisher sat, having disassembled his M4 carbine for cleaning.

"The privates are back. They look like shit," Joe said.

"Badger," Fisher said, "that guy makes me sick to my stomach. What are you up to, anyway?"

"Gonna catch up on some reading."

"Got some books from home, Manny?"

"Yeah. I'm reading a book by Paul Auster. You can read it when I'm done with it. So far, it's good."

"Alright, Manny. Talk to you later."

13

Fisher could not sleep. They had been in Iraq for 75 days. He lay on his bed at JSS Medina and wrestled with his thoughts.

This is when it would be easy to give up.

Most of his uncles were locked up when they were his age. The government conducted experiments on them in Holmesburg Prison and Eastern State Penitentiary, and Graterford Prison. Fisher intended to break the cycle when he joined the Army straight out of high school. He was on his third deployment in six years.

There was nothing complicated about sleep deprivation. One simply became so exhausted that the brain was forced to switch to autopilot. The mind took to wandering off on its own occasionally. Before joining the Army, he entertained an idea about joining the Night Stalkers of the 160TH Special Operations Aviation Regiment. Flying helicopter missions for Special Forces. He wanted to do something out of the ordinary. Instead, his Army test scores upon qualified him for a job as an armor crewman, although at the time he did not even know what that was.

Fisher got a firsthand view of the invasion in 2003 through the periscope of his driver's station aboard an Abrams Tank. He learned everything he could as fast as possible, especially concerning the turbine engine that guzzled fuel. It was the job of the driver to be intimately familiar with the performance characteristics of the behemoth, and Fisher was an eager student. He knew how fast his tank could go in forward or reverse, how deep it could ford water, and when its automatic transmission would shift gears, depending on the pitch of the engine's revolutions. With his extensive knowledge, he could push his tank around, over, or through just about anything in its path. If he couldn't, then it couldn't be done. By anybody.

Long gone were those days from the invasion, and the rules of engagement that enabled soldiers to use their weapons candidly in the cause of victory and self-preservation. The Surge was more nuanced, designed to surgically root out the enemy while embarking on a doctrine that was supposed to gain victory over the insurgency by transforming the conditions that fed into it. That was too much bullshit to get his head around. The purpose of an Abrams tank was to destroy, and the tank did not discriminate. It would kill its own crew if the opportunity were to present itself, as the lessons of history had proven.

Insurgents, on the other hand, were more predictable. They required specific conditions to accomplish their mission. The urban wasteland of southwestern Baghdad was not a chessboard for the Americans to test their counter-insurgency doctrine. This was a game of checkers, a brutal war of attrition and willpower.

The tankers went out again, on a smoldering August night. It was a tank patrol. Intelligence reports had begun to paint a portrait of the enemy. He preferred to stay close to his targets. Trying to move personnel and equipment for an IED strike required passing checkpoints or, more dangerously, running coincidentally into Americans on patrol. The game was checkers, where the players only moved their pieces one block at a time.

Baja Company's compound in the middle of Al-Jami'ah was too small to accommodate tanks. Even if it were big enough, the colossal amount of fuel required to keep the machines running would have turned the old schoolhouse into a suicide bomber's dream. Out of practicality, the tank missions always embarked from Camp Liberty. As the vehicles rolled out of the camp, the thrash metal sounds of Annihilator blared over the headsets within Lieutenant Redd's tank. His role was to exercise command and control over a vast quantity of mobility and firepower.

A platoon of four tanks with full combat loads could carry a total of more than one-hundred and forty rounds of ammunition for the main gun, which was a 120mm cannon that could dependably reach targets as far as four kilometers away. In addition, the platoon boasted eight 7.62mm machine guns and a whopping forty-five thousand rounds of ammunition. Each tank commander had at his disposal a Browning, .50-caliber machine gun and a prescribed combat load of nine-hundred rounds of ammo. Added together, a platoon of four tanks loaded with ammunition looked to be an escort for the Grim Reaper himself to anyone that might catch a glimpse of the spectacle as it creeped by, under the cover of nightfall, on the prowl.

Playing by the rules of the game, the platoon drew near Medina, slinking along the quiet streets like four giant, sand-colored slugs. When communication was necessary between the tank crews, it was done so in a whisper over the radios. The platoon split into two sections and infiltrated a residential area.

At Medina, Captain Davis relayed information between an intel source and the tank platoon. It seemed he had waited without end for that moment to arrive. The tank platoon proved itself to be resourceful over the summer, operating outside of its element by conducting countless foot patrols and acquitting itself to the task. The source of the information was deemed reliable by higher echelons in the chain of command and passed down to Zach Davis for exploitation. Lieutenant Redd's tank platoon was on the move, ever so slowly. It might be the night to register a kill.

The moment for action drew near. Everyone in the tanks heard the hushed voice of Captain Davis, giving information to the platoon leader about an IED being installed at that very moment. Joe was the loader on Lieutenant Redd's tank. From the description given over the radios, they were less than a kilometer from a group of insurgents digging a hole in the ground. Tanks, barely moving, one track pad to the next so that inside, the crew felt the bump-bump-bump of distance creeping along.

Lights out, no talking. Communications were limited to hand and arm signals. Past an Iraqi Army checkpoint in the road, about eight-hundred meters from the target.

The tank leading the patrol was commanded by Staff Sergeant Badger, in charge of the wingman tank for Lieutenant Redd. Using thermal optics, his crew spotted a group of men digging a hole in the road up ahead, about five to seven people in all. Curfew was in effect, so it was apparent they were up to no good. Off in the distance, Apache helicopters circled, looking for their own shitheads to kill. The Apache crews confirmed what the staff sergeant in the lead tank could see from his vantage point, a distance of six-hundred and ninety meters away. They were spying on an IED being emplaced.

Just behind the staff sergeant's tank, Lieutenant Redd's tank set, hunkered down, in the middle of the Iraqi Army's checkpoint. The staff sergeant's vehicle was barely fifty meters ahead, Badger's hushed voice breaking radio silence as he communicated with the Apaches nearby.

The platoon leader relayed the observations of his wingman's tank to the company's command post at Medina. Clear indications of the enemy's hostile intent toward coalition forces: Checked that box. Under the rules of engagement, deadly force was authorized. Lieutenant Redd, on behalf of his wingman, requested permission from Captain Davis to engage the enemy. The staff sergeant had maneuvered within six hundred meters of the IED emplacement team.

Elijah Redd requested permission to go "hot" with the tank's main cannon, utilizing a canister round packed with enough high explosives to blast hundreds of tungsten balls scattering down the street. At that range, the shot would have scattered considerably, but still close enough to wipe the enemy off the face of the planet.

Moments of silence followed.

Captain Davis granted authorization to engage with crew-served machine guns only. If the tank platoon were to be successful, it would have to rely on the accuracy of the gunner's 7.62mm machine gun. "Engaging," the staff sergeant's voice announced over the radio.

Tat-tat-tat-tat-tat-tat

Silence followed as the echoes of the machine gun died off.

"Red One, this is Red Two, negative B.D.A..."

Joe had watched from his loader's station when the tracer rounds emitted from the wingman's tank into the empty darkness toward their intended target. The Battle Damage Assessment revealed nothing but failure, no enemy targets hit. In the gloom of night, the desperation of the moment sunk into his chest.

The shitheads got away.

He had taken the Army at its word that, when the moment of truth arrived, soldiers would get to send the shitheads to their God. But they were robbed of their opportunity. A canister round would have done the trick; collateral damage be damned.

What the fuck are we doing here?

What were they supposed to tell Briggs, or the comrades whose pieces they picked up and put into bags that night in June? They had the enemy in their reticle and lost him.

The tanks rolled up to the IED site. Fisher got out of his tank and hopped down. He picked up a shovel and slammed it onto the ground.

"This is bullshit!" Fisher screamed, looking at Lieutenant Redd. "If they want tanks out here, let us do what we fucking do!"

"Get back on your tank, Fisher!" the platoon leader shouted.

"No problem here, sir," Fisher responded bitterly, climbing onto his tank. "Let's keeping driving around with our thumb up our ass. No problem." Fisher sank from view into his tank.

Joe was halfway out of his tank, watching. He turned to his right and saw Lieutenant Redd, and their eyes met. "My wife's not gonna believe this shit, sir," Joe said, putting a wad of tobacco into his mouth. "I guess we won some hearts and minds tonight."

Joe extended the can of dip to the platoon leader, who grabbed a pinch and put it in his mouth. "We could have got them with that can round," Elijah observed. "Yup, that can round would have done it."

"Well, if they send us back, we can make it in time for midnight chow," Joe said. "This scene is cold anyway. At least some of them Haji motherfuckers probably shit themselves in the pants."

The platoon leader laughed. There was nothing more that could be done except call it up.

"Baja Six, Red One. Negative enemy contact." Afterward, the tank platoon conducted a presence patrol around Al-Jami'ah. The streets were dark and serene. The taste of soot was in the air from something unseen, burning in the quietness.

They traveled uneventfully throughout the sector. The roads were stark, stretched out before the tanks. Each soldier was apt to pass the time in what manner came to mind. One might zone out to the music through a headset or try to pick apart the mission's failure. They were playing the enemy's game on his turf, under a different set of rules. Everywhere there had been an unholy mess of minds and bodies, broken across the beaten path laid before them. Unexpectedly, they reached the advent of a new phase in the fight. A gate had swung open, and they faltered.

All around, the darkened buildings seemed to mock them in silence. The night had made buffoons of the out-of-towners. The patrol took them to places that were familiar, but as if new to them. When dawn came, the birds would proclaim them as washouts. All the fresh corpses on the sidewalks would belong to their shame. Everything around them was without hope. The high spirits that carried them in from Kuwait were gone.

When the patrol was over and the equipment was stowed, Joe sank into his bed at Camp Liberty. From his head to his boots, he was drenched in sweat. The stench of exhausted soldiers filled the tent. He searched himself for the rage that had been his companion, at times threatening to send him over the edge. It had left him. Had he been wrapped up in some idea that had been fed to him, perhaps? The enemy seemed capable of striking at whatever time and place of his choosing. The feeling within him was like a substance, tangible but without a name. He could still see that shock in everyone's eyes when Briggs got hit. Then a feeling there was a score to settle, but when? Now, the priority was only to stay alive. Joe knew by heart the doctrine of counter-IED operations. At times he could not remember the names of the four soldiers that were killed by the bomb that went off just a few months before, and that was a feeling stranger to him than anything else.

14

Briggs was back in Georgia, the home of the 3rd Infantry Division. He had been driving back to Fort Stewart after two months of convalescent leave in Oklahoma when a Georgia State Trooper pulled him over for speeding and smelled alcohol on his breath. He was arrested for Driving Under the Influence and ordered to attend Alcoholics Anonymous meetings.

It was like a slap in the face. Three months after an improvised bomb in Iraq left him with a metal plate in his head and a jagged scar on his neck, he was forced to sit among a group of strangers who talked endlessly about how hard it was to stop drinking. Whether he went to meetings on post or off, he was sure to run into other soldiers in the rooms. Not that it mattered. He had seen many soldiers test positive for marijuana or cocaine. The Surge was in full bloom, and the Army was throwing bodies into the fight. Enlistment qualifications had been relaxed to the point that convicted felons were being admitted into the Army, especially if they wanted to join combat arms. A conviction for drunken driving was nothing more than a bump in the road.

Being on convalescence in Oklahoma that summer was a retreat from life in the Army. He went to stay with his dad and stepmom in Lawton, where he had grown up fishing the banks of Lake Ellsworth. He unpacked his rod and reel from the attic, took his dad's boat out of the garage, and returned to the lake. On the water,

Briggs steered the boat toward wherever the shad were schooling on the surface. Seagulls hovering overhead gave away the shad, which were a sure sign that white bass were underneath, hunting for food. When the bass were scarce, he took a heavy rod and reel, rigged some punch bait to a large hook, and cast the bait into the water, letting the line flow from the reel as it sank to the lake bottom as much as fifty feet in depth, where Channel Catfish and Blue Catfish swam about, searching with their barbels for something to eat.

Briggs started each fishing expedition from the same boat ramp. Nearly every time he set the boat in the water, there was a female wood duck with her brood of a half-dozen ducklings. They stayed in the shallows, nettling the water's surface with their bills. Reliable as clockwork, they went about their business while he eased the boat off a trailer and into the water, parked his truck and set off to spend the morning hours fishing. He left his phone in the truck.

It was the first time in years he could be alone, which he wanted more than anything. When it was time for lunch, he took the boat out of the water. Briggs would go home, clean and fillet his catch, and put away the fish in a freezer. After eating, he would read from *Close Range* by Annie Proulx. Then it was off to bed for a nap. It was a good way to spend the summer before going back to the Army. Just as the calendar turned to September and the first week of dove hunting was in season, he was already back in Georgia.

The drunken driving charge and mandatory Alcoholics Anonymous meetings were a can of worms he had to deal with for sipping on a whiskey bottle on the trip back East. He usually kept a bottle of Old Crow in his pickup truck for an occasional taste. The journey to Georgia was twelve-hundred miles and lasted two days, and it started the morning after the Oklahoma Sooners opened the college football season with a win over North Texas. Briggs woke up that Sunday morning and had breakfast at the house with his dad and stepmom, then drove up to Oklahoma City, turned east onto Interstate 40 and crossed into Arkansas at Fort Smith and kept driving, following the Arkansas River all the way to Little Rock, where he had dinner and checked into a motel. He had stocked up on bottles of Old Crow to keep from running dry on Sunday, when hard liquor was not for sale. Not one to get roaring drunk, Briggs was content to sit in the comfort of a chair, sip his whiskey, and click through the channels with the remote control to see what the good people of Arkansas were watching on television that night.

He tried to stay out of his own head. Sometimes he wondered what happened to the girl he had married nearly ten years before. They were married a few weeks out of high school and then Briggs was off to basic training. The cycle of training and combat tours in Iraq were too much for Nicole Briggs, so she packed up her belongings and left their house in Georgia during her husband's second deployment, in 2005. Austin Briggs could not be served divorce papers while he was downrange, but his stepmom gave him the news after reading the public notice in the local newspaper back home. He had no ill feeling toward the girl. She never did him a wrong turn, as far as he knew, and he was away from home most of the time.

On a Monday, Briggs slept in for as long as possible and checked out of the motel in Little Rock before being charged for another day. He was back on the road and made it to Memphis in time for lunch, then checked into another motel. The trip from Little Rock to Memphis took only two hours. He would be back to the Army soon enough, but he had plenty of money in the bank from his tours in Iraq, and he was in the mood to enjoy himself. Except for New Orleans, there was no place like Memphis. He listened to jazz and the blues, walked around the downtown scene, and enjoyed some of the best food in the country to his liking. Seafood was his favorite. The sounds and flavors carried him back to the motel, where he cracked open a bottle of Old Crow and watched television.

Amid the moments of comfort, he felt within him a darkness brewing like a storm. Memories of being covered in the blood of his fellow soldiers would intrude, whether he was sleeping or awake. He would dwell on the frustration he felt while looking in the night for their body parts. Sheltered in the safety of a motel room, Briggs wrestled with guilt, having let everybody down. They were still in Iraq while he enjoyed his sinful nature, taking his fill of music, food, and alcohol, before going to sleep on a soft bed. When he slept, he was often startled awake by voices of soldiers, screaming inside his mind. He would wake up and peer outside the window, searching the parking lot below for signs of activity. Then he would check the door to make sure it was locked before sitting in a chair and turning on the television and drinking his whiskey until he was numb. Rage would well up inside him, and he would punch walls and lamps, finally taking out a large knife from his bag. He would heat the knife with a lighter, then burn stripes into his forearms and torso. The pain seared his mind, temporarily blocking out the hysterics of his turmoil. Only then could he regain his focus and feel settled, like he was in control.

Then it was time to go back and he was on the road, making his way from Oklahoma to Georgia. He was almost back at Fort Stewart when a state trooper pulled him over near Statesboro, and Briggs failed the field sobriety test.

As much as he disliked the individual and group sessions on combat stress before going on leave, Briggs found the Alcoholics Anonymous meetings even more unpleasant. They were run by people who claimed to be sober for years, and Briggs found them to be uppity in their achievements, their happy days of abstinence.

Summer days spent fishing followed by nights sitting on a porch under the Oklahoma sky were memories. Back to the reality of Army life in Georgia, he dutifully attended the meetings as ordered by the court. At a weeknight meeting in Savannah, he listened to a middle-aged Hispanic man he had seen around Fort Stewart. Briggs recognized the soldier as a senior enlisted man from the 3rd Infantry Division, but he could not recall where he had seen him, it had been so long ago. The man was dressed in gym clothes and leaned forward in a metal folding chair.

"It's been a hard weekend. I never felt it this bad," the man said. "I thought I was cruising by, but it was just one thing after another. My headphones didn't work at the gym, and I just snapped. I was on the heavy bag for about forty minutes straight, trying to relieve some stress. The rest of the day I just felt myself urging. I haven't ever felt like that, and it was bad. I feel quick tempered, and so I have a heavy bag at my house to blow off some steam. I went to it, like, four times throughout the weekend. It was tough for me this weekend. Even last night, I slept for about two hours. The nightmares came back. I felt like there was a big sound and somebody grabbed me, so I flipped over and fell off the bed. After I got up, I couldn't get back to sleep, so I got up and ate a whole bag of cookies. That's why I couldn't get back to sleep, because I ate a whole bag of cookies with milk at four o'clock in the morning. That's bad too, because I was doing good with my diet and I broke it while eating that, so I felt worse. Usually when that happens, I just drink, but I can't drink anymore."

Briggs tried his best to focus on what was being said. He rejected the idea that he may have a drinking problem, but he begrudgingly respected people he encountered at the meetings, as they spoke openly about their troubles. But upon hearing something familiar, his mind wandered. He had difficulty sleeping for years. Whiskey enabled him to fall asleep, but he was restless and awoke often, and when morning came, he was always exhausted.

"You're not the only one about the dreams lately," somebody said. Briggs looked up and saw a younger man, probably in his early twenties. "I been dreaming hardcore lately. Waking up, getting pounded on the back. That's keeping me up at night sometimes, too. Cravings for me have been horrible lately. I really kept myself busy last weekend so that wouldn't happen, at least I tried some things. You're not alone with that, so if you need somebody to talk to outside of here, just give me a call."

The leader of the meeting was a woman who appeared to be in her fifties. Wearing a summer dress with flowers on it, her brown, wavy hair streaked with grey as it hung down to her shoulders, her face tan and wrinkled, she looked like a Georgia country girl, alright. She arrived at the meeting behind the wheel of a late-eighties, Jeep Grand Wagoneer, brown in color with woodgrain paneling on the sides. She butted the remnants of a cigarette she had been smoking and made her opinion known.

"The important thing is that even though he struggled, he didn't drink, and he made it, right? He made it, but it's really hard," she said. The woman seemed to lack the air of superiority Briggs sensed in the many of the other old timers.

Another man in the room spoke up. "My old lady, we threw a party this weekend. She didn't want to leave me in the living room because we had some friends over and they brought some wine. After they left, there was some left over, and she poured it out."

"She knew you were struggling," the woman in the flowered dress suggested.

"Yeah, she noticed," the man replied.

"So, she poured it out," the woman said. "That's what we talk about in stress management, so, good job. Not for feeling that way, but let's you and I talk later and see if we can figure out what other pieces are going on to make you feel that way, okay? Who wants to go next?"

He at once had a peculiar feeling about the meeting. It seemed as if he had stumbled upon a private group that shared intimacy, and he was an intruder, an uninvested voyeur in a world where people were really trying to do something with themselves for the better.

"It's the Labor Day weekend, and I always struggle with long weekends," said another man who appeared to be a soldier in his early twenties. There were few women in the meeting of about fifty people who packed the small building, which had previously been a liquor store many decades prior to being bought by a local Alcoholics Anonymous chapter. When Briggs heard that story, he was convinced those people had been around the bend with alcohol a few too many times.

The young man continued. "I think they signed out on leave, that's what it was. I packed my stuff to go to a concert back home. It was a country concert, you know? It was excellent. I pulled up in my dually, I had my boots on. I went home a little later than I wanted to. It's about a four-hour drive to Tallahassee. I wanted to leave at five and get there by nine, but I had to stop and get some gas, and I forget what it was, but I had to do something else. So, I got there late. I woke up early too, because I haven't been able to sleep either. I'm asleep then I'm awake and waking up earlier. I don't know what it is. It's not nightmares, I just wake up in the middle of the night and I'm wide awake. Anyway, I woke up around eight and I wanted to go for a run, then I went to this old gym we used to go to back home. I went back home and ate some doughnuts. That's what I hate about going home. I always eat so bad. If I'm not eating at Waffle House, I'm eating what my mom makes. I eat tuna for about a week straight when I'm at Fort Stewart, then I go home and eat cheesecake and Waffle House. That's why I don't like to go home for about a month or two, because I pig out and that's not helping. I'm getting a gut. I saw some of my old friends. I went to play soccer near Lake Jackson. I played horrible."

After a pause of several moments had elapsed, it was clear the man was finished. Out of nowhere, a voice in the back of the room rang out.

"It was that Waffle House!"

Laughter filled the room. Briggs used the distraction to get up and draw another cup of coffee from a pot that sat on a nearby table. He pulled a five-dollar bill from his pocket and put it into a plastic cup next to the coffee pot, then stepped outside to be alone.

15

Captain Davis was enjoying a moment of peace at Camp Liberty. The hottest days of summer were behind them. Because of this, he allowed himself the pleasure of resting in a comfortable chair in an air-conditioned, hangar-shaped building run by the Army's Morale, Welfare, and Recreation service. He had seen the hardships of The Surge during the first ninety days in Baghdad. Bodies of his soldiers were torn apart by IEDs. Baja Company showed its resilience, its platoons going outside the wire every day, rooting out the enemy, making him reveal his tactics.

The Army had published *The First 100 Days*, a handbook that discussed military operations in Iraq. The book was always in Zach's cargo pocket. It came from soldiers who were surveyed in an attempt by the Army to figure out why casualties were so common in the first one-hundred days of a combat deployment. Most impressive to Zach was the enemy's adaptiveness. Ever keen to the Americans' manner of executing their plans, the enemy proved himself capable of blending improvised bombs into the local landscape and detonating them for maximum effect.

IED attacks left forensic evidence, and Zach's soldiers were on a mission to search every building in their sector, looking for signs of enemy activity while talking up the civilian non-combatants, trying to win them over. Eventually the scales seemed to tip in favor of the Americans, but Zach could not say just when that happened. A phone number for anonymous tips led directly to Medina, and the calls began to trickle in as soon as his company arrived and started going door to door, saturating the streets with its presence.

Zach was reminded of *Army Life on the Western Frontier*, in which the Army's inspector general, Colonel George Croghan, visited garrisons and reported on his findings in the twenty years leading up to the Mexican War. When dealing with Indian affairs, Colonel Croghan was vexed in the fall of 1827 by the plight of the Osage Nation, which was threatened by its enemies, the Pawnees. By the colonel's estimation, the Army could preserve the Osage and bring stability to the frontier territories of Kansas and Oklahoma although, he emphasized, "An infantry man might as well be sent to chase the elk or deer as to pursue the Osage or the Pawnee of the Plains."

Zach was mindful of the Army's conquest of the Great Plains when he found himself brooding over the complexities he discovered in Baghdad. The Army tried to placate the Native Americans with money and gifts almost two hundred years beforehand. In Iraq, it was a similar strategy, funneling money and political influence toward anybody the Army found useful in quelling the insurgency and sectarian carnage. Finally, he found a chance to rest and reflect. Nearby the infantry commander was a group of his tankers, watching a replay of the championship fight between the Mexican super bantamweights, Israel Vázquez and Rafael Márquez. The tankers had gathered for a watch party, their most rambunctious leaders being the lively Latinos, Joe Cuero and Fisher Santana.

Zach closed his eyes and listened to the banter of the tankers, as the two fighters engaged in a rematch in Hidalgo, Texas. His tankers were on their best behavior when at the Forward Operating Base of Camp Liberty, but at JSS Medina, in the middle of Al-Jami'ah, they walked around in shorts and sandals, with their rifles slung over their shoulders as if on a hunting trip. They were a motley bunch of soldiers, but they proved their mettle in the dogged, hot months that summer.

"Márquez is gonna break that kid's nose again!" Cuero shouted, as both fighters traded punches in the third round, opened cuts on each other's faces, and blood flowed from both combatants.

"How's he gonna do that? He can't fucking see with all that blood he's leakin'," Fisher shot back. He had an unlit cigar in his mouth and removed it to give vocal support for his fighter, Vázquez.

The group of tankers was a boisterous lot, voices bursting forth in cursing and shouting, celebrating and taunting among themselves. Zach could see the large-screen television from his corner of the room. Both fighters were bleeding heavily, pounding away at each other. Several in the group admonished the new kid, Stillwater, for getting up between the third and fourth rounds to go outside to use the latrine. "Hurry the fuck up! You might learn something here, new guy!" one of the tankers hollered, inflaming a cacophony of laughter from the others at Stillwater's expense.

"Don't shake it too much, Manny" Fisher said, "I don't like piss all over the seat."

"Hey, Stillwater, make sure you sit down when you piss, alright?" another advised. The suggestion generated another round of laughter as the private walked out.

Zach closed his eyes again. Half the size of an infantry platoon, the tank platoon was just as raucous when its soldiers had free time to themselves. Outside the wire, they lacked the firepower and tactical proficiency of a platoon of infantrymen. It bothered Zach that some of the tankers were overweight, to the point of being unquestionably out of shape. Their uniforms were often dirty, and they went for days without shaving. All in all, they made for an unseemly bunch of characters.

In terms of appearance, the new kid, Stillwater, looked to be the most squared away. Probably why they hounded him so much, hiding his weapon, or sending him to the mechanics in search of parts that did not exist, such as boxes of reticles. Upon arriving in Baghdad, Zach had directed each of his infantry platoons to donate a soldier to the tank platoon to beef up its numbers. That was a mistake. The platoons took the opportunity to get rid of the lowest of their bottom feeders.

The tankers were at their best when they were on the tanks. They used powerful, thermal-imaging systems to detect emplaced IEDs. Moreover, the tankers were adept at sending concise, accurate reports that painted a picture for the commander as to what was happening within the area of operations.

With the waning days of summer came a glimmer of hope for Al-Jami'ah. An unflinching American presence, along with a strategy of engaging key leaders in the area, bleeding the energy out of the insurgency. Violence was dwindling, replaced by a resurgence in the market districts. The tankers had a hand in that success, and Zach was proud of them. It could not have been easy for them, being removed from their tank company and plunked down into a company of infantry grunts. Keen to capitalize on the success, Army brass wanted to keep the tanks off the streets in favor of a friendlier, lighter footprint in the region. The prospect of giving the tankers full-time duty on foot patrols caused Zach some anxiety. If they were to be successful, they could use an experienced hand. More importantly, a proven operator who could be counted on to lead by example if a mission turned upside down. He was going to give them Chopper.

Chopper had a reputation for being a meat eater. A killer. The enemy's worst nightmare. Any insurgent that crossed paths with him got his ticket punched. He was a man free from the emotional entanglements of conscience in all matters but, most notably, in combat. He grew up in Madison County, Florida, where he briefly attended North Florida Community College before withdrawing to enlist in the Army on September 11, 2001. With a quick trigger finger and a capacity for violence, Chopper would fit in well with the tank platoon, giving it the spirit it needed. Satisfied with his decision, Zach eased deeper into the comfort of the padded chair.

One of the tankers bellowed, "That Mexican's got some big punches, yo!"

"Manny, what the fuck you talkin' about? They're both Mexican!"

Howls of amusement intruded upon Zach's thoughts. Then tankers were at a fever pitch as the boxing match raged on, both fighters pummeling away at each other.

"Hey, Manny," Fisher informed Joe after Vázquez dropped Márquez with a solid punch in the sixth round, "you gonna owe me a fiddy."

"No way, it ain't over yet." But it was. Márquez was beaten by an ensuing flurry of punches as the referee stopped the fight, and Vázquez avenged his loss in the first fight a few months earlier. The Texas crowd on television roared its approval, and Joe reached into his pants pocket to retrieve a wad of cash for Fisher. "Okay," Joe said. "Here you go, asshole. If there's a rematch, I got Márquez again. You down?"

"Yeah, Manny. They got another fight. Maybe your boy can get your money back."

"Hey! Shut the fuck up over there!"

It was Staff Sergeant Badger, looking up from a book he was reading on the far side of the room, by himself. Their fun cut short, the tankers went outside to smoke and talk shit, as always. The night offered a cool breeze. They exchanged insults one final time before the group broke apart, some headed to the dining facility for midnight chow, others back to the tent for sleep. Fisher and Joe lingered for a while, examining the night sky in silence. Stars were clustered about like the drunken footsteps of an alien spirit that had passed by eons ago. Both soldiers shared an unspoken inquiry at the vast blackness overhead. They accepted their insignificance within the spectacle; their own mortality but a comedy amid the cosmos enveloping them. Their presence merely corrupted the elegance of the universe.

Back at the sleep tent, Fisher lay on his bed, a feeling of amusement coming over him in the darkness. He pulled from his pocket the fifty dollars Vázquez had earned him. "Fucking Mexicans," he whispered, placing the cash back in his pocket. "They got big nuts."

He reached under his pillow and pulled out a Smith & Wesson pistol. It was from the spoils of a weapons cache the platoon had stumbled upon a few days prior. Fisher had found the semi-automatic pistol and, as no one was watching, tucked it inside his body armor and out of sight. He was going to disassemble the weapon and smuggle it back home when the deployment was complete, but that was months away. Fisher had a SIG Sauer back home in Philadelphia. That gun cost him almost a month's salary. Like his SIG, the bootleg gun he kept stashed under his pillow had a polymer frame. It weighed just over one pound, and it felt good in his hand. He ran his fingers over the weapon, admiring its balance and design.

"You're a sexy little bitch," he said softly.

He was ambitious to use it. The strain of the deployment was keeping him awake at night. He was sent to a psychiatrist to talk about combat stress, but he wanted none of the lecture that old man was preaching. He was living one minute to the next, no time to think, only to react. Previous deployments had convinced him of that, and the combat tour this time around was the same story. No reason to listen to a shrink who wanted to crawl up inside his head.

Enemy contact was a daily occurrence when the platoon hit the streets at the start of summer. Other than Briggs getting hit, the platoon stayed healthy. The trucks and tanks had been damaged regularly but the mechanics always patched them up and got them running again. The shitheads weren't crazy enough to get into a gunfight. They wanted to blow shit up and fade into the shadows. Fisher could see the enemy advancing along a trajectory that could have only one outcome, and that was defeat. The Army was not going to allow a bunch of ragheads win this fight.

America's capacity for evil was perverse. It used members of his family like human guinea pigs in prison experiments. More than anybody in the platoon, he could appreciate the government's persistence in achieving its objectives. America was a cruel genius. At the approach of dawn, Fisher fell asleep. He slept through the morning hours and awakened in time for lunch. The platoon had been granted a day of rest at Camp Liberty. Its leaders set out a plan to conduct maintenance for the Humvees.

The break was a chance for the platoon to meet Chopper. An introduction was not necessary, as everybody had heard of the infantryman's exploits outside the wire. On his platoon's first mission, an IED attack in broad daylight stopped their column of Bradley Fighting Vehicles. Soldiers hastily dismounted and, seeing an Iraqi on a street corner documenting the scene with a video camcorder, Chopper opened fire with his M249 Squad Automatic Weapon (SAW), tearing the man apart with his light machine gun.

That was Chopper. Outside the wire, his brain worked at an accelerated rate that tended toward violence of action. In the blink of an eye, he could ratchet up the bloodshed to an astonishing level. The term, "tactical patience" was not in his vocabulary. Between combat deployments, Chopper earned his Ranger tab but was not assigned to a Ranger battalion, largely because of his numerous run-ins with law enforcement. He was entrenched in the ranks of the lower enlisted soldiers, and he was fine with that. As soon as he was downrange, he offered no headaches to his leaders, many of whom agreed he was among the best soldiers they ever had, but not one they would allow in their homes for a weekend cookout.

Tankers greeted the newcomer heartily. The existence of a known meat eater in their ranks was welcomed with sincerity. Chopper's arrival sent a wave of enthusiasm throughout the platoon. It was not the only good news that day. Word spread through the platoon that Briggs had been cleared to return. In a few weeks, he would be back in Iraq.

Everything seemed to happen in a hurry such that Joe could not keep track. He remained in contact with Briggs by way of occasional emails. Summer crawled almost to a halt at times. Joe missed having his mentor around to make sense of it all. Briggs was a steady influence within the platoon. When the shit was piled so high Joe wanted to scream, there was Briggs, with his practicality and calm demeanor, lending advice and diffusing problems with a few words.

Good news of the moment seemed to suggest the platoon had reached a bend in the road. A storm had passed, washing away the scorched summer. At times, it seemed everything was going to collapse. A hint of optimism returned. Trust was renewed. For all that had been lost, it was time to settle in for another fight. Put to an end the enemy and his will to continue.

16

Briggs sat across a table from a middle-aged man with a scruffy, handlebar mustache and wire-rimmed glasses. The man read from *As Bill Sees It*, a collection of writings from one of the founders of Alcoholics Anonymous that was published forty years prior. He read from page thirty-seven, a verse entitled, "A Full and Thankful Heart," which was first published in 1962.

"I try hard to hold fast to the truth that a full and thankful heart cannot entertain great conceits. When brimming with gratitude, one's heartbeat must surely result in outgoing love, the finest emotion one can ever know." The man placed the book down on the table and removed his glasses. Austin was one of just four people at the Sunday night meeting of Alcoholics Anonymous held at the old liquor store.

"This is one of the reasons you should write a gratitude list," the man said, looking at each of the three men seated around the table. "The reason that needs to be done from time to time is because sometimes we all get sideways about things. We tend to get materialistic. We didn't get this, and we're a little pissed off, or something else is going on to where we didn't get what we wanted, how we wanted, when we wanted. Making a gratitude list is something you do in good times and when you're not right. You're grateful that you've got a roof over your head. You're grateful that you've got a running car that doesn't give you any trouble."

It was October and hot summer days of Georgia had gone away. Austin had knocked on enough doors and pissed off plenty of high-ranking officers throughout the chain of command until they finally relented and agreed to send him back to Iraq. The shrapnel wounds to his head and neck had finally healed, and he was cleared medically to get back into the fight. He had stayed in contact with Joe and Fisher on the goings on in Baghdad, and with each report of the platoon being attacked with improvised bombs, Austin could barely hardly contain the emotions that had him wrapped up inside and closed off from the world around him. Every night he went to sleep wondering what the platoon was doing at that moment. IED attacks were still a regular occurrence, and that new guy, Chopper, seemed to be trouble waiting to happen.

The Alcoholics Anonymous meetings that were mandated by the court were about to come to an end, just in time for him to catch a flight back to Iraq. He was filled with rancor at the enemy, and he wanted personal revenge for his injuries. To keep himself occupied, he traded in his pickup truck for an old Cadillac. The pearl blue, droptop Caddy had 472 cubic inches of big-block motor under the hood. Briggs let go of a piece of what he always thought should be in the eyes of others. He could visualize every detail, cruising the strip in Las Vegas with the top down, his left arm on the steering wheel, his right arm over the shoulder of a gorgeous man. Dressed to nines and looking suave. Walking around the best casinos wearing an Oxford suit and Italian shoes. He had exerted himself all his life, trying to work out, on his own, the idea of being gay. Whether in the culture of the deep south in Georgia or the ardent conservatism of the Great Plains where he grew up, he could not figure out what it meant to be himself.

It began in June 1994, when he was fourteen years old and just out of middle school in Lawton. His baseball team had won a big game, and the coach invited them to his house and treated them to beer and pizza. It had been a great day, winning the tournament championship for their age group. Like Austin Briggs, most of the other boys on the team were having fun. It was the final summer before high school, and they were going to make the most of it. Drinking beer and eating pizza, they felt like men. Coach Henry taught American history at high school and coached youth sports. Furthermore, he was thought by the teenage zeitgeist of Lawton to be a living paragon of modishness not seen in the other adults in town. He had an inground swimming pool, and some of the boys jumped in, laughing and rollicking in their drunken state. From nowhere, the boys were passing around a fat, bulging joint, and the smoke ebbed into the languid, night air.

When it came to him, Austin inhaled deep and slow, filling his lungs, the necromantic voodoo working its way into his mind, blending his cognizance with a new, enchanting awareness of how things are. The alcohol and weed made a gala reaction in Briggs. He stood by the edge of the pool, swaying pleasantly to the tantric melody of "Wave of Mutilation," by The Pixies. Without warning, somebody jerked his bathing trunks down to his ankles and pushed him into the pool. The other boys laughed off the prank and went about their merriment.

The coach had a Jeep Renegade parked in the driveway. He had a two-story beach house with a view of Lake Ellsworth from the second-story balcony. He often hosted parties for his baseball players after big games. Parents were fond of the coach for the emphasis he placed on the development of individual players over team wins, although the latter came in abundance. The coach's wife had died from cancer years earlier, and parents saw the relationship between the coach and his players as mutually beneficial.

Austin slumped into the comfort of the Jeep and closed his eyes. The universe was an ambrosial theory, twirling in his head, making him dizzy. He lost consciousness. After a time, he awoke to a spasmodic orgasm. He lay there in the passenger seat, listening to crickets and locusts far off, then opened his eyes and turned his head toward the driver's seat. Coach lit another joint. Austin had an intrusive notion that his parents might be concerned about him, as it was well past midnight. But he could not gather himself to say a word. He accepted the joint that was offered and took a hit.

In the most subterranean hiding places of his mind, he knew what had happened. If anybody saw the coach going down on him, he was so buzzed and happy at that moment, he did not care. He had a crush on his coach for some time, but he could not make sense of it. Austin let the smoke curl from his mouth. He was starting to get hungry. On the street, there was nothing. They drove to an all-night burger stand. Between the munchies from the weed, night swimming, memories from the baseball game, skinny dipping under the night sky, he was in an altered state.

He wrangled with his emotions for years over what happened that night. It set him on a wild excursion in search of himself through his years in high school, carousing with girls, beer parties, playing football, getting into fights. Nothing could obliterate the notion of queerness he feared. It was like claustrophobia.

Maybe he drank too much to cover the feelings, mask his feelings of inadequacy. At six-and-a-half feet tall, he was the center of attention playing football. He could catch, tackle and block, but he was slow of foot and not much of a prospect to play in college, although he did get some interest from small schools in Oklahoma, Texas and New Mexico. It was what he was expected to do, yet he had no interest in it. Instead, he made up a tale about trying out for Special Forces when he enlisted in the Army. It turned out Army life was not what some made it out to be, and he did not apply himself toward much of anything. The rank of sergeant eventually fell in his lap, only because he followed orders. By the time he rolled into Baghdad in early 2003, he had already been busted down because of his attitude. He watched people die, some of them by his own hand, in those hectic days of war in the combat zone.

Years passed by. When his contract was up, they put reenlistment papers in front of him, and he signed them without giving it much thought. The Army had something to do, it kept him away from Oklahoma, and it put money in his pocket. Austin admired the others in the platoon. They seemed to have a purpose, while all he had was direction. Going on ten years in the Army with nothing to show for it but some scars, a Purple Heart medal, and having to listen to those drunks talking like they were philosophers.

In a way, they had a sweetness about them. They were trying to get somewhere. The man with the handlebar mustache in charge of the meeting had a gravelly voice and an indomitable spirit to boot, like he was going to stay sober and take as many drunks as possible with him on his quest. Austin had to smile at the man's determination.

"You woke up this morning," the man said. "You're still breathing. You woke up sober. You've got another day. There's a lot of reasons to be grateful that, sometimes, we forget. To this very day, I will get sideways about things. Some things drive me crazy. Sometimes what we want and what we have are two different things. Suddenly they come together, and I see the wisdom in what I did or why it happened the way it did."

Austin's mind was cast about in every direction. Since his injury, it was hard to stay mentally focused for more than a few minutes at a time. It was as if his brain was digging itself out of a hangover the morning after a bender. There were instances when he would awake at night from a vivid nightmare. He had nightmares before, but these were on a new level of realism that left him lying in bed, sweating, and filled with dismay.

If he could get back to Iraq and back on the streets with his platoon, things would return to normal. He wanted to get back to his job as a gunner, sitting behind a machine gun in the turret of a Humvee, protecting soldiers that were working on the ground, vulnerable to the enemy. It was a shame his guys had to see him the way he was when he got hit. How timidly they led him to the truck for medevac. The trauma surgeons that were waiting for him at Balad had seen much worse. Austin knew he was in good hands with them. Still, it seemed they rounded up everyone they could to gather around while the docs worked on him. The discomfort that came with being naked and gawked at was worse than getting tagged by the enemy. He knew he was messed up, but the spectacle was too much for him.

Meanwhile, handlebar mustache was going on about many adventures in the rooms of Alcoholics Anonymous. Austin was developing a growing fascination with the meetings he was required to attend. Whether the people he met truly shared a disease or not, he was not qualified to say. But they were crazy, he was sure of that. They did not talk of big ideas, nor spin wild stories. It was the way they let oddball ideas slide as mere footnotes into conversation.

"… not much longer after that, my dad got his Agent Orange disability, so I was able to quit college and go into drinking full time."

What the fuck did that guy just say?

17

Jerry Payton awoke in the dark, early morning at Medina. It had been a restless sleep; less than two hours. It was time to start the day. He brushed his teeth and walked down the hall to the command post. As the senior enlisted man of Baja Company, First Sergeant Payton answered only to Captain Zach Davis in his role as the company commander's top advisor. Jerry also was the company's enigma. Nobody knew his hometown. He preferred it that way.

During his first decade in the Army, he spent time in Panama, Saudi Arabia, and Rwanda. His personnel file was scrubbed clean of many of those places. His days of jumping from airplanes and rappelling from helicopters were old memories. He spent more time overseas than at home. Not surprisingly, he was on his fourth marriage. There was a chance the new wife might stick around. Before heading to Iraq for The Surge, Jerry had turned in his retirement papers and was set to be a civilian for the first time since Ronald Reagan was the commander-in-chief. But the Army had instituted a "Stop Loss" policy, meaning he had one more trip to the sandbox before he could retire.

A commotion brewed within the compound. The tank platoon had captured an insurgent. It was quite by accident, really. The tankers were on a routine patrol when they happened upon a group of Iraqi soldiers that opened fire on a crowd of men caught in the act of emplacing an IED. All were shot to death but for one, and the survivor was tossed into the trunk of a Humvee and brought to Medina, where he was placed on his back, blood pooling all around him, writhing in agony.

It was the first time Joe had seen the enemy. The man looked miserably frail, with ashen-colored skin, his eyes glassy as he laid there, going into hypovolemic shock on the concrete floor. The Iraqi interpreter was relaying questions to the man from Captain Davis. A cluster of infantrymen had gathered to observe the interrogation.

It reminded Joe of his youth, when his family would go to South Padre Island for summer vacation, and he saw people hanging around the fishing piers to see what the charter boats had caught. His family rented a house there each July, the week after Independence Day when the summer season was in full swing.

Looking down at the man that had been shot, Joe felt betrayed by the sympathy that seeped into his conscience. The voice in his head that said what he was looking at wasn't right. Fuck that, he told the bothersome voice. The shithead on the floor may have been involved in the IED attack that killed his four brothers from Baja Company, and on top of that, the sonofabitch might have been responsible for Briggs getting hit. Briggs had just come back to the platoon, and he stood there next to Joe, watching the interrogation.

Joe could not ignore the legal questions as to what was occurring. He thought of the analogy of a tree falling in the woods. If nobody said anything about the situation, did it happen? It seemed they had come too far and seen too much to let this fish get away. It wasn't likely anybody was going to rat about the incident but, even so, if the man on the floor, shot multiple times through the legs, was an enemy combatant, the Americans were required to give him medical attention. Nobody was doing anything except watching, and so Joe went along with silent consent. The combat medic for his platoon was standing by, looking on indifferently while smoking a cigarette. They were crossing a line, but they did it together, without saying a word or asking even one question. It was happening and nothing was going to stop it.

Maybe it was payback for all the success the shitheads had against the Americans throughout the summer. Without medical attention, the man was likely to bleed out right there on the floor. He wasn't giving coherent answers to the questions Captain Davis was asking. The wounded man begged for water and mercy. Contempt for the man showed on the faces of the infantry soldiers that stood around him. They appeared ready to tear him apart, if afforded the chance. Yep, Briggs had to be pissed off at the sight of it, Joe was certain. Not because the medics weren't working to keep the man alive. Briggs would have a hard time making sense of trying to get information from a guy bleeding to death. That was Briggs' nature that required the ends to justify the means, and what was taking place that morning had neither logic nor reason.

"Hey, Manny. You got a cigarette?" Fisher asked Joe. The request drew the attention of everyone. Joe reached into a pouch that was fastened to his body armor, pulled out a pack of Newports, and handed it to Fisher. Sometimes Fisher did things at the most awkward moments.

Fisher lit the cigarette and walked past Captain Davis, then stooped over the man on the floor, making eye contact with him. "Hey yo, Manny, you wanna smoke?" Fisher asked.

"Who the fuck do you think you are?" demanded one of the infantry soldiers, rushing toward Fisher and grabbing him by the throat. He was a well-built staff sergeant, with forearms as thick as a man's neck. Fisher broke the man's grip with an overhand right that caught the infantryman by surprise.

"Fuck you, nigga!" Fisher shouted, as he flailed another wild punch with his right hand. In a tumult, soldiers converged into the scrap. Punching, shoving and cursing merged into a flurry and then broke into packs of combatants, with their red faces, bloody noses, swollen lips, and scraped knuckles swaying in a convoluted mass of humanity that was fighting and swearing amid a whirlwind of dust, frustration, and resentment.

"You keep asking this guy questions," Fisher said, breathing heavily while struggling against the weight of several soldiers holding onto him. "I don't wanna bust your balls, sir, but you keep asking questions, he gonna tell you he was part of the attack on Pearl Harbor," Fisher continued. "He's fucking bleeding out."

Captain Davis glared at Fisher. The commander had no patience for insubordinate conduct. Just because Fisher's assessment was correct did not give him a pass to speak out of turn. Anything the insurgent gave them would be better than the intel being provided by higher echelons. The real, no-shit intel was given to Special Forces operating in sector. Whatever information they got from the insurgent, they were going to keep in house and pray it would pay off. The dustup had subsided but for a few half-hearted shoves between tankers and infantrymen. First Sergeant Payton leaned against a Humvee, a Bahia Brazil cigar jutting out of a wide grin that spread across his face.

"That's what I'm talking about. Keep it going, I love it," he said.

"Hey, Fisher, let me have a word with you," Captain Davis said. Fisher walked with the commander toward a corner of the compound. Lieutenant Redd accompanied them, seeing as how he was the platoon leader and Fisher's insubordination was a direct reflection of his leadership. The three of them stood silently for a few moments with the morning sun barely over the horizon.

"Not gonna make a big fuss over this, Fisher," the commander said, "but let me be clear. I won't have it, plain and simple. This isn't your first time over here, so you know how it works. This guy might not give us nothing but shit, or maybe he'll give us shit and the name of another guy. Now, if we're lucky, maybe we'll find that guy. And really, that's all I've got to go on, and that's all I'm gonna say. Don't you ever undermine me again."

"Yes sir," Fisher said, and walked away, leaving Captain Davis and Lieutenant Redd.

"What the fuck was that, Elijah?" Zach demanded.

"I'll fix it, sir," the junior officer replied.

"No, you won't. When it comes to good order and discipline, that's NCO business. First Sergeant Payton is having a conversation with your platoon sergeant right now."

Elijah looked down at the ground and let the words of his commander sink in.

"Summer school's over," Zach said solemnly. "We put a dent in the insurgency, but with the weather cooling off, Haji is gonna come out to play. What do I always tell my lieutenants? Tactical patience balanced with violence of action. We're not anywhere near done with this thing, Eli."

"Yes sir."

Captain Davis turned and headed for the main building.

"And what about the punch?" Elijah asked.

"What punch?" The commander said. "I didn't see a punch."

"Roger, sir."

Captain Davis walked back toward the crowd of infantrymen and the captured insurgent. "Oh, by the way," he said, looking over his shoulder without making eye contact. "Chopper is going out with your platoon today."

The platoon left Medina later that morning on a foot patrol. Early autumn was somewhat cooler than the stifling summer heat in their first few months in Iraq. The outer perimeter of the compound was a concrete wall with a height of twelve feet. Once outside the wall, they were in a highly populated, residential neighborhood.

Their exit from Medina was through the only way in or out, which was on the north side of the security station. From there, they turned immediately west and skirted the perimeter, with the security station to their left and a vacant lot to the right. Once clear of Medina, they spread into a formation known as a staggered column, with a file of soldiers on each sidewalk and the platoon leader and platoon sergeant in the middle of the street. Each soldier maintained an interval of at least three to five meters from the closest man to him. The platoon continued its westerly move with Briggs leading soldiers in a file on one sidewalk and Joe on the other. They walked the measure of five football fields before coming to a T-intersection.

Briggs held up his right hand and balled it into a fist, which signaled the platoon to halt its movement. Joe mimicked the hand signal, hunkered down to one knee and leaned against a wall for cover. He scanned the area ahead, wondering what got Briggs' attention. It was the middle of the day and the street was empty. Something was off. Joe was aware of his heartbeat quickening.

"You got something, Briggs?" a voice called out from behind them.

Lieutenant Redd and Staff Sergeant Badger ran forward until they reached Briggs, who was crouching next to a car parked by the sidewalk. Joe searched the windows and rooftops nearby, looking for anything that might have caught Briggs' eye.

Joe was aware of darkness and a deafening, high-pitched ringing in his ears. Face down on the ground, he tried to prop himself up but could not move. His gloves were covered in blood and black soot. He heard the muffled voice of Stillwater.

"Hey, he's moving! Cuero, stay down, man. Stay down. Don't move. We're gonna take care of you."

Joe rolled to one side, grabbed his handheld radio and keyed the mic. "Baja X-ray, Baja X-ray," he groaned. No response. He was aware of several men scuffling around him. Someone was screaming

"Medic!" Most likely he was going to die, he realized. This was what it must feel like.

"You're gonna be alright, Cuero." a voice said. It might have been Stillwater, but it was like hearing a voice with a pillow wrapped around his head, so he could not be sure. "Listen, Cuero, we're going to put you in the truck and get you out of here."

"Don't bunch up," Cuero replied. "Pay attention, Stillwater. Is that you? You okay, Stillwater?"

"Yeah, Cuero. I'm up."

"Good. Keep scanning. Where's Briggs and Fisher?"

They placed Joe on a canvas stretcher and took him to the truck. He turned his head while he was being carried. Everywhere there was dark smoke, but he saw the body of a soldier whose face was gone. All that Joe could see was charred, blackened flesh that was torn apart. Soldiers picked up the lifeless body and carried it to another Humvee. He saw a group of soldiers gathered around something on the ground, but he could not see what it was through the bulk of humanity. He heard voices bellowing with fury.

"Where's Briggs?" he asked, as he was loaded into the truck and the door closed.

He awoke and sat up. He was in a hospital bed. The platoon sergeant's face said it all. Sergeant First Class Young told Joe there was an IED in the car that blew up next to Briggs, Lieutenant Redd, and Staff Sergeant Badger. They were gone, and so was Captain Davis, who was killed by another IED later that day. And just like that, they were gone. It was a planned series of attacks against the Americans, the Iraqi Army, and local police that day.

The tank platoon returned to Camp Liberty, having lost a quarter of its soldiers in the blast that killed Briggs, Badger, and Lieutenant Redd. And then there was Chopper, who went crazy and started shooting when the IED exploded. He opened fire on a nearby car that was driving past, killing a teenage boy who was in the wrong place at the wrong time.

Joe was diagnosed with a closed-head injury. He was sent to the Landstuhl Reginal Medical Center in Germany. The doctors told him he had a severe concussion. After a few days there, he was taken to an airfield and sent back to the United States.

18

You wake up one day wondering where the time went and realize it's over. Maurice Young retired in 2014 at the rank of master sergeant, finished his degree in architecture from Kennesaw State, and moved to Texas. Passion for his field of study struck when he was stationed in Germany and traveled throughout Europe, studying buildings in England designed by Philip Webb.

By the time of his retirement, he had been to four combat tours in Iraq in eight years, with three deployments with the 3rd Infantry Division from 2003 to 2007, and a fourth hitch with the 1st Cavalry Division out of Fort Hood at the start of Operation New Dawn in 2010, when he was sent to the northern city of Kirkuk.

Born and raised in Georgia, Maurice found a second home in Texas with the 1st Cav, where he ended his twenty-four years of service. Rather than accept an assignment as first sergeant of a tank company at Fort Hood, he elected to hang up his boots. During his final dozen years in the Army, he was either downrange or having surgery on bones and ligaments that were bent and worn down by life as a tanker.

The Surge took a little extra from him, and he could not get it back. Maurice was going through the motions in the years that followed. Too long before he realized he should have retired sooner. He had paid his dues long enough.

When the Army approved his retirement request, he had two months of leave coming to him. He went with Chloe on an extended vacation. For the first time in his life, he went to places as a visitor, not as a soldier. They started in Israel, waking up every morning to panoramic views of the Mediterranean Sea and the Carmel mountain range. Then on to India for two weeks, visiting temples, taking in the vast array of architecture, and rediscovering their own spirituality. From there they made their way to Vietnam, and toured the local markets, ate street food, and went on extensive walks in the countryside. After two months of holiday travel, they were ready to return home and grow old together.

Texas was full of wide-open spaces, where a person could be alone. Maurice preferred it that way. As his time in the Army was winding down, he ventured into areas west of Fort Hood and began flipping properties with his wife. Their financial posture was secure after all those deployments and the frugal nature of Chloe, who saved every nickel of the hazardous duty pay he earned. The woman had as much grit and guts as any Army wife, putting up with his night terrors and mood swings whenever he was back home. For Chloe and Maurice, their first successful flip was a small, one-bedroom house on ten acres of land near Lometa. Their enterprise quickly took off, as they bought properties in Kempner and Lampasas, did much of the work themselves, and pocketed the profits. By the end of Maurice's enlistment, their net worth was nearly a half-million dollars.

When it was time to find a place that suited them, they had a home built on twenty-five wooded acres outside the city limits of

Lometa. Maurice sat on the back porch before dawn, sipping hot coffee and planning his day. He and Chloe found a trusted business partner to handle the contracting for their properties, which freed Maurice to spend his time outdoors.

In the summer, he went fishing and bird watching. In the fall and winter, he was in the woods and fields, hunting. He owned a phone, but Chloe would not let him have it. After he retired, it rang incessantly. Former subordinates and peers of his would call at all hours of night or day. Finally, Chloe had enough and whisked the phone out of his hand in mid-conversation. "You're out of the Army," she scolded. "They need to figure out what's what on their own."

And that was the last Maurice ever saw his phone. He stayed in touch with some people, though. His wife was unaware he had a Facebook account. On occasion, he would go back to Fort Hood to have lunch with one of his old buddies or host them for a hunting or fishing trip on one of his properties. He found it familiar that some of them expressed regret over something that happened in the past. It was strange to his thinking, mostly because it confirmed he was not the only one having feelings of guilt.

A feeling that something was wrong hit hard when he went to Fort Hood to meet up with one of his old tanker buddies. Devon Bryant was from the bayous of Louisiana, and his fellow soldiers had called him Shadow on account of his dark skin. Shadow was proud of his military lineage. His ancestors were from Ohio, and several of them went to Massachusetts to fight for the Union side in the Civil War. Maurice met him when they were both sergeants during the Thunder Run into Baghdad. Afterward, Shadow went from one duty station to the next, and they stayed in touch by phone and email over the years.

When Shadow retired around the same time as Maurice, he relocated to Texas and landed a job as a civilian for the Department of Defense. He gave classes to soldiers preparing to get out of the Army, trying to pass along his knowledge to the soon-to-be civilians. Maurice accepted his friend's invitation to sit in on one of the seminars, after which they would have lunch and catch up on old times. Maurice sat at the back of the classroom while Shadow lectured on how former soldiers were seeking healthcare through the Department of Veterans Affairs.

"In the event you might get sick, you have a way of being treated," Shadow told the group of about forty soldiers. "Case management. These are the people…let's say, for example, you're assigned to your hospital and, within the hospital, you're gonna be on this team, under this doctor. When you start going and seeing this doctor, you don't feel comfortable. You just don't feel comfortable. You don't, I don't know, for whatever reason. You just go back, tell case management, I would like to be changed from, get another, a different doctor. No question asked. The V.A. will be sure that you receive…they want, they want you to be, feel comfortable, when you come, and you receive medical services."

Maurice sat in the back of the room, dumbfounded. Shadow had been an articulate man, with an authoritative presence, in his element when it came to public speaking. He had devolved into a nearly incomprehensible mess. At the front of the room, Shadow pressed on with his speech.

"Recognize and address your mental, uh, excuse me, your mental health needs. Your emotional well-being is especially important, considering the growing numbers of people diagnosed with depression as well as issue of suicide. The V.A. believes every suicide is a tragic outcome. Regardless of the number or rate, one suicide is too many. The V.A., it will do whatever is necessary to provide a way of anyone to contact, and receive, information in regard to any emotional issues. The V.A. wants to be sure we all have a way of communicating, because it's everywhere now. It's, um, the numbers are too high still, but this is as much as we can do. We can reach out and be sure that when anyone calls or uses that information, those receiving the call or the message, those are people that work, either related to the military branch or, somehow, a nurse, someone that is an expert in that area. So be sure that you do so. We just wanna be sure that you're taken care of."

Maurice's gut reaction was to rush out the door and not look back. He could not have been the only person in the room to be uncomfortable with the presentation. He pondered the thought as Shadow continued with his delivery.

"Vet centers offer adjustment counseling and a wide range of psychological services so you can make successful transition from military to civilian life, and that's basically what they do. For some of us, going from…after so many years of, um, military service, going back to being you again is gonna be easy. For some of you, it's not gonna be so easy. It's gonna be bumpy. It's gonna take time to adjust at the house. Some of us are not at home that often because of the mission. Because of everything we do, the many hours we spend outside the house. Pretty soon, once you finish, depending on how fast you be able to get a job, will determine how many hours you gonna be at the house now."

Maurice was overcome with a burning sensation in his head, the familiar migraine headache making its way up the back of his skull and advancing toward his eye sockets. He pulled the medication out of his pants pocket and swallowed them with a gulp of water from a fountain in the hall, then returned to the classroom in time to witness Shadow stumbling his way through the conclusion of his speech.

"Sometimes your partner doesn't take it easy," Shadow said, eliciting nervous laughter from the soldiers in the audience. Most of them seemed to be as uncomfortable as Maurice, watching the scene unfold. Shadow seemed to be the only person in the room oblivious to the unnatural, staccato state of mind he was putting on display. Simply put, he was all over the place.

"Sometimes it's gonna be rough, because there's no one to give orders now, and I'm not sure if they're gonna be willing to take orders from you. So, if that's the case, if it takes time to adjust, that's why they've been created, the vet centers, to ensure that they provide. And on the same page, it provides the different types of counseling they provide. Individual and group counseling, family and marriage, bereavement, uh, referrals, post deployment, health reassessment, substance abuse, employment screening for referrals, uh, as you can see, the many ways that they ensure that we can readjust back to be us again. So be sure, if it comes to, that you need their help, be sure you do, you do so and, uh, and receive those services."

Afterward, Maurice and Shadow had lunch at a Mexican restaurant. They hardly spoke to each other during their meal, then parted ways. The experience drove Maurice into a gloom, unlike anything he had ever known, and it lasted for weeks before Chloe could pull him out of it. He sat on the back porch at predawn every day, his cup of coffee next to a stainless-steel revolver. The Ruger was chambered in .44 Special and had a three-inch barrel. It was his backup whenever he went outdoors. His primary weapon was a work of art, a Beretta 12-gauge with a bronze receiver, chrome-plated trigger, and rubberized butt pad. The semiautomatic shotgun was loaded with ribbed Brenneke slugs. When Maurice went hunting for big game, he wanted to be close to the animal for a quick, merciful kill. The combination of firearm and ammunition, together with proper shot placement, assured him that his quarry would not long suffer. He carried his weapons afield even when he was not hunting. Coyotes and feral hogs were always around his property and being armed granted him a sense of security.

Solitude was his companion. Whether hunting or fishing, he was usually alone. He could take a break from himself. He was taking sessions in art therapy. His love was designing buildings, which he and Chloe were working toward over the years by fixing up houses and speculating on land for profit. But in art therapy he was caught by surprise, expressing himself through sketches depicting his nightmares. His mind was disoriented, looking at the finished product of his work after the first session. He had been thinking about looking at the present through the prism of the past. The art therapist taught him how to bridge the gap between previous experiences, the feelings associated with them, and the way things really were.

Maurice realized he had been living a secret, that he was afraid of success, existing in a world of frustration and anxiety; unsure, yet all the while aware how well things had been going in his life after the Army. Sometimes he wondered if he would ever sort it all out.

He went out one morning to his grand champion of properties, nearly sixty acres of sparsely wooded land with a wet-weather creek running through the terrain. He had taken a large, white-tailed deer there the previous winter. The buck had a thick neck and massive antlers. The eight-pointer was the biggest in the county that season, and the kill garnered Maurice some local fame, which he intended to leverage in the sale of the property.

On that summer morning, he was searching for a kestrel hen that was raising a family amid a stand of oak trees. He took with him his shotgun and pistol, as well as a Nikon camera with a telephoto lens, in hopes of spotting the birds. In the grass by the oak stand, he found one of the young birds. Its eyes were hollowed out, eaten by ants that had made their home in its carcass. They scurried over and into the body, seeking further nourishment from the fledgling raptor. Maurice squatted and placed his shotgun on the ground. He closed his eyes, searching within himself for a prayer. For a while he set there until the words came, not from a pulpit, or the Bible. He recalled a Hindu veda he learned in a college course, years ago, on world religion. He staggered to his feet and spoke softly:

For a thousand-day journey the wings of the yellow swan
Are spread abroad as heavenward it flies
Gathering all the gods into its bosom, it
Flies on, surveying all the worlds.

19

Fisher had the Marlin rifle his dad gave him for his eleventh birthday. He used it for hunting deer each winter. Otherwise, the old gun stayed perched above a fireplace at home. The Pennsylvania woods were full of natural wonders. It was Labor Day weekend, and he drove an hour north from Philadelphia, then east through Quakertown until he arrived at Nockamixon State Park, in northern Bucks County. Fisher went there or, sometimes, to nearby farms where he had permission from landowners to hunt groundhogs and scout for signs of deer in anticipation of the coming season right around the corner. He hunted deer during archery season in October, and antlered deer with his rifle in November.

When hunting groundhogs in late summer, Fisher wandered, exploring the woods near fields cultivated with alfalfa and corn, looking for small trees where bucks had scraped away the velvet from their new antlers. It was the ancestral ritual of autumn, when does went into estrus, sending the bucks into a manic rage to fight each other, competing for hierarchy in their quest for does with which to mate.

The morning air was dank, even before the sun came up. Fisher locked the front door of his row home as he left. He considered going back inside and returning to bed with his wife, Leslie. But she had given him a ration of shit the night before, about going hunting while a list of chores had gone unattended most of the summer. The woman had a kind nature, and she was merely playing with him, for the most part.

Fisher left the house wearing faded jeans, work boots and a tee shirt, and a white bandana folded into a headband that he wore across his brow to keep sweat from stinging his eyes. He carried a small ice chest. In the cooler, there was a pastrami sandwich that was cut into quarters, batata fritas, and some tostones. He also carried a large thermos filled with iced tea as he climbed into his truck.

Interstate 476 took him north to a farm less than an hour from home. He brought a new Hornady rifle. The gun was topped with a Leupold riflescope, and he was curious to see how the combination of weapon and optic would perform out to two hundred yards. A fence line led him to a familiar place that overlooked an uncultivated field, and he set up his equipment under the cover of a red pine tree. The tree provided little shade, but it was better than lying under the blazing sun.

Fisher scanned the grassy area below with a spotting scope. He spotted a pair of big groundhogs near some scattered rocks, but they were at least three hundred yards away, out of range. For a while he watched them as they nibbled at the grass, moving occasionally. Feeling a grumble in his belly, Fisher opened the ice chest and removed one of the sandwich wedges. He placed aside the spotting scope and sat with his back to the tree for support, then unhinged the prosthetic limb where his lower left leg used to be.

He tilted his head down so that his chin was tucked against his chest and let out a faint laugh, thinking about that badass, Captain Davis. The Hispanic soldiers called him the Cisco Kid, and

First Sergeant Payton was known as Pancho. It was an inside joke among the soldiers. One of the endless, dumb things that came about while being in close quarters with each other for long periods of time. There were no hard feelings about it, but nobody dared let the commander or first sergeant in on the running joke, either.

Fisher kept in touch with Joe Cuero, who was living in Austin, Texas, and their old platoon sergeant, Maurice Young. The Surge took everybody else. Of those that made it back that Fisher was tight with, several were either killed in subsequent combat tours or suicided themselves in the years that followed.

Maurice said Fisher was looking for spirituality after he got out of the Army. He encouraged Fisher to keep a daily journal, and he did, for a while. Fisher was medically retired after getting his leg blown off during The Surge, and his friends said he should just let Uncle Sam pay the bills. But he wasn't having it. He knew he would go crazy sitting around, doing nothing.

Sitting in the shade as the morning passed, he pulled a blunt packed with red-haired sensimilla from a plastic bag he had stashed in the ice chest when Leslie wasn't looking, and he lit it. The hillside was quiet while Fisher sipped cold tea and got high under the pine tree. He fell asleep. A light breeze awoke him, just in time to see a male wood duck flying through the cloudless sky.

He packed up his things without firing a shot and returned home to Leslie. They went to a matinee at a movie theater, then to dinner at an Italian restaurant in South Philly. When they got home, they walked around the neighborhood. Past the stickup kids that roamed about, the dealers selling dope, and those looking to buy.

Cars with out-of-state tags lined the street, their occupants eager to cop and get the fuck out of there, go anywhere, and get high. Fisher loved everything about the rawness of the North Philly badlands, its obnoxious filth and beauty with an electric tension to it all.

They climbed the stairs to the rooftop deck he built after leaving the Army. Even with one leg, he was as good a carpenter as anybody. Leslie made sangria with oranges and white rum, and they reclined in padded lawn chairs to sip and look at the skyline.

"What're you thinking about, babe?" Leslie asked.

Fisher smiled. "Thinking about Briggs. He would've been giving me shit today, passing up on those fat hogs."

Leslie laughed softly. "You're just like Maurice, going out into the woods with a gun knowing every animal out there is safe. Why don't you get a camera and take it with you, like he does?"

"I might," Fisher replied.

She was right, as usual. He passed on several opportunities that day in the field. Same as always, but he wasn't ready to splurge on a photography kit just yet. Like Leslie, Maurice had encouraged him to get one so they could compare the Pennsylvania wildlife with that of Texas. Maurice thought that was a fine idea, and Fisher agreed. They kept correspondence by writing letters. It seemed Fisher's old platoon sergeant was doing well in his retirement and that was good. He earned it, having put up with Fisher and Briggs for three combat tours. A few months back, they were reminiscing about Briggs, and Elijah Redd and Zach Davis, as the ten-year anniversary of their deaths came and went. What a bunch of hardcore, professional soldiers to have had the honor of serving alongside, they agreed. It was a sad occasion, upon realizing ten years had passed. So much so they decided that Fisher would have to get his ass down to Texas, where they would track down Joe Cuero for old time's sake. Maybe run around Sixth Street in Austin with the college kids, act like fools and get good and drunk. They read each other's letters and laughed out loud, reminding each other of all the crazy shit that happened downrange. Leslie, for her part, at times thought Fisher had gone right out of his mind when he handed her Maurice's letters and she read them, shaking her head as Fisher looked over her shoulder, read along with her, and kept giggling like a little boy.

Leslie preferred to see him this way. Better than the version of him that kept coming back from combat. Each tour, he got worse. They fought. He was irritable at his best, and at his worst he would fly into a rage. In his sleep, he would choke and hit her. One time, she left the house and stayed away all summer. She had given so much that she lost herself along the way.

That was a few years back. He was drinking heavily, and when he got drunk enough, he would stay up all night and watch videos of people getting their heads cut off on the internet. She thanked God their kids were grown up and out of the house. Against the pleading of her friends, she moved back in, but only after he started seeing a psychiatrist. Leslie's strength was enough to save them both. Fisher never forgot that. She was everything. If they had gone their separate ways, he would probably have died. It wasn't such a crazy idea.

Staring into the sky, he was at ease. He was grounded in rational thought, which required letting his wife know when the conversations in his head were going toward the dark, as Briggs used to say. At any given time, Fisher would veer off into sadness and depression. He took medication prescribed by his psychiatrist, who was ambivalent about Fisher smoking marijuana but did not give him too much grief about it.

Leslie reached over and caressed his neck with her fingertips. "Maybe after these drinks, you can take one of those magic blue pills," she purred.

"I think maybe I'm too old for you, little girl."

She got out of her chair, placed the glass of sangria on an end table, and took his hand. "We'll see about that," she said, leading him toward the bedroom.

20

Joe had back surgery to fix damage sustained over the years. The recovery took six months. He went for a walk twice a day at the beginning. School was back in session from kindergarten through college. The Labor Day weekend was an afterthought as a holiday. In Texas, the real happening was the start of the high school football season, which started in late August. He lived in a small, two-bedroom, A-frame house in Austin. Viviane had left him. He felt lost without her and detached when she was around. It was a long drive to his assigned duty station at Fort Hood, but he had undergone back surgery and with another procedure to repair his neck coming up, he was rarely required to be at work.

He went shopping at an outlet mall in Round Rock. He bought three shirts from a Hurley store: two tee shirts and a buttoned short-sleeved with palm trees on it. He lost the Hawaiian shirts she had gotten for him when they were dating twenty years ago. She would go to Penner's in downtown San Antonio. The Army moved them around so much he eventually lost track of them. Mostly he wore old tee shirts and jeans, and it bothered her. She said she wanted him to stay occupied and sober, and so she encouraged him to buy himself clothes, camera equipment, and to keep writing. He had some poetry and a short story published, and she practically dragged him to poetry readings so that he could share his work. The woman was insufferably magnificent at times, despite leaving him. He could hardly blame her.

After surviving The Surge, Joe stayed in the Army for the next ten years and made a career out of it, which took him around the world a few times and got him promoted to sergeant first class. Just like Maurice Young, he became a platoon sergeant and molded young officers and Noncommissioned Officers. He was coming toward the end of it.

He had occupied his time over the summer by reading Leonard Gardner's novel, *Fat City*. It was routine for him every Tuesday. Mondays were spent washing laundry and cooking red beans and rice. Aside from that, he stayed at home and worked at keeping busy. He had been involuntarily admitted to an Army psychiatric ward at Fort Hood on two occasions, where the staff told him their role was to stabilize him rather than treat his "unspecified manic-depressive disorder."

A few days after his surgery, he went back to work behind Viviane's back. He intended to check his email and print a few documents, but it just so happened that Equal Opportunity representatives from the battalion and brigade were visiting with the company commander. It was a big deal. Periodically, the Army would conduct surveys to gauge the "climate," of the commander's Equal Opportunity program.

Joe was the EO representative at the company level, and he was already aware of several red flags that were raised in the most recent survey. Some of the senior leaders that had been identified as problematic in the recent survey had never crossed the line with him, and some of the negative comments had, in fact, come from him. The Army was never going to be a level playing field. He had been an EO rep long enough to know the chain of command was going to do as little as possible to address whatever concerns were raised in the survey. It was an exercise of futility. Without a smoking gun, such as a senior leader showing up for work dressed as the Grand Wizard of the Ku Klux Klan, nothing was going to change.

He decided to take a trip to Florida. Just got in his car and left, driving almost twenty-four hours straight to Sarasota. The summer was over so there would be fewer people at the beaches, since he hated being in crowded areas. While on the road trip, he realized he was stuck in a lot of *shoulds*. It was difficult to focus on recovery. As soon as he got to his hotel room, he uncapped a bottle of Hendrick's gin and went about drinking himself under the table.

The next morning, he awoke to a throbbing hangover and the realization his life was a catastrophe. He resisted an urge to text Viviane, unsure of the damage he had caused the night before. It was a blur. After checking out of the hotel, he drove almost an hour south to Manasota Key, checked into a beach house, and went for a swim to clear his head. Later he had lunch and returned to the rental with a bottle of rum to get smash-faced drunk. He took some Excedrin with the alcohol to lessen the next hangover. Willpower was out the window.

It was wishful thinking that Elijah Redd was still alive so that Joe could buy a postcard and send it to his old platoon leader and lie to him, tell him everything was okay, and he was enjoying himself in the Florida sun after the tourists had gone home for the summer. Instead, he sat on a bed with his back to the headboard and pillows, a bottle of rum in one hand and a handgun by his side. Holding the weapon and knowing he could stop the pain whenever he wanted gave him a woozy sense of comfort when he was lonely.

Another hangover. It was Sunday. He was done with all of it. The time had come to go home. He got on the road about lunchtime, and it was about eight o'clock in the evening when he stopped in Pensacola for dinner. Then the journey took him through Alabama, Mississippi, and Louisiana under the cover of nightfall.

Every time he stopped for gas and food, he went to the restroom and saw his face in the mirror. There was no place he could go and nothing he could do to change it, or the monotony of it all. He arrived home at mid-morning Tuesday, got cleaned up, and ate. A flashback hit him while doing laundry. Their first time in Iraq; sent in to sift through the aftermath. When they arrived at the scene, it seemed the devil himself had come to visit. A Humvee flipped upside down in flames. So much blood and death in the air, it tasted like a dirty, iron spoon had been shoved in his mouth.

They stayed there about eight hours, recovering body parts, pieces of weapons, and sensitive items. How weary he felt that night. It was all so repetitive, as though they had been there before. The night was dreary grotesque, and just another night outside the wire. Just like when Briggs got killed. In the aftermath of being attacked, the desire of wanting to kill people, but unable to pull the trigger because of the rules.

Things could change. Hell, they always did. Whether he would be able to focus on himself and let the marriage take a back seat, he did not know. He was old-fashioned, for one thing.

He dedicated himself to a therapy plan that started with swimming laps at an indoor pool before dawn each day. It seemed reasonable that what was happening inside his head would eventually stabilize, that he would be happy, or content, but it was not yet happening.

He awoke several times each night, and it was a struggle to get back to sleep. He stopped drinking. He was nervous most of the time. Viviane was different and so was he, and while they seemed to have some chemistry together, there was an edge to it that felt awkward. He cooked pasta and she came over to the house. They ate and watched a movie. When he anticipated things would turn out bad, they usually did. She had asked him whether he was going to continue his therapy if she went through with the divorce. It would not be an easy thing to do, but the alternative scared him.

Oftentimes he left the house for a walk and tried to find peace of mind. It was difficult to focus on anything, but at least he was out of the house. Nothing seemed to count for much. He awoke early on a Saturday morning, looked at his watch, and it was two-thirty. At that moment, Viviane texted him. She could not sleep, either, asked if he wanted to go shopping later. Everything was good for a moment, and then it was dragged back down again by something unseen. The depression was overwhelming.

He was swimming laps the next morning when it came to him. If he could focus on just one thing each day, maybe that would be enough. Not that he could focus on one thing all through the day, but when his thoughts became jumbled, he could come back to that one thought, and that would help him get back into the moment. He focused on his writing, and the next day he worked on a video project. He had created a YouTube channel. If the act of remaining engaged could keep him from dwelling in irrational thought, then maybe that could be a start. After all that had happened, he had to let it go. He was not sure how much he could. If he could let go of one thing, it would not even matter what it was, just that he had taken a step in that direction, it might be a new start.

21

Maurice said he was going to Huntsville to witness the execution of Robert Lynn Pruett. His friends asked what business of his was it, whether Pruett was guilty of murdering a prison guard, or not? He was already serving a sentence of ninety-nine years for his involvement in a murder in Nueces County. But Maurice never offered an explanation. He had seen many people die, mostly because of him carrying out orders. Everybody had to pay up eventually. This time, somebody was going to meet death, at a time and place already chosen, and that was it.

The execution was set for the twelfth of October, and so he left a few days early on Monday, driving south to Austin, where he had breakfast, then east all the way to Hempstead, in Waller County.

Maurice brought his discharge paperwork the Army had given him and burned it at the gravesite of a notorious Texas Ranger named Henry Lee Ransom, who was shot and killed at a hotel in Sweetwater. Ransom's marker was a plain, grey slab with his name and an inscription: Died - 1918.

There was a reason in his mind for what he did, but he didn't tell anybody because they would not understand. He read about Ransom and what he had done during the Bandit War in the summer of 1915, in a book, *The Texas Rangers and the Mexican Revolution*, by Charles H. Harris III and Louis R. Sadler. Ransom killed an attorney in 1910 and was acquitted. He was appointed chief of police by the mayor of Houston two years later. He was demoted after allegations of brutality and eventually went on to work as a manager of a prison farm. Ransom was commissioned as a captain of a Texas Ranger company during the Bandit War, where his infamy as a callous lawman spread throughout the Rio Grande Valley. And there at the site of his remains, Maurice stood over a small slab of marble. A man's life is done and marked by a stone. It was as good a place as any to end something, like the Army discharge he burned right there at Ransom's grave. He had carried those papers around with him for a long time, first out of a feeling of necessity. After a time, it seemed he just held onto them when he had no need to, and when he would stumble upon them it caused him to think about the afterlife, having killed and even tortured people to accomplish the mission. He was hell bent and foolish, and the feelings about the things he had done stayed with him. The Army went on without him, as some people said it would. There was nobody to blame. Soldiers do whatever needs to be done to bring their buddies back home. Those were the things he heard from families and friends, the kind of polite talk that gives everybody a clean way out of something.

He knew one thing for sure, that he felt lousy inside every time he came across those papers. Maurice thought maybe the Army turned him more hardhearted in dealing with people. He was a soldier with an ability to disconnect his emotions. His reputation for keeping his wits in combat was well known among his seniors, peers, and subordinates. But the character of his conduct brought with it the notoriety of having a cold, calculating regard for human life, whether enemy or comrade. It was because of this that Maurice found kinship with people such as Henry Ransom. History books do not write themselves, after all. Governments and politicians tell their versions of history. People like Ransom get no say in the matter.

Maurice didn't think of himself as anyone special. The experiences he had downrange were already written by others. When you're gone, what difference did it make, anyway? He left the Army behind because the ride was over. He stood there and watched the paper burning to nothing on the ground. When finished, he went to a Mexican restaurant in Hempstead, ordered enchiladas from the lunch menu, which included beans, rice, and pico de gallo.

After lunch, it was a short drive north on Highway 6 until he reached Navasota, where he checked into a Victorian style bed and breakfast and had dinner. Navasota was the birthplace of bluesman Mance Lipscomb, who Maurice and Chloe often listened to on their porch during the Texas summer nights.

The next day was Tuesday. Maurice awoke before dawn to the clanging of a wind-up alarm clock he had set to five o'clock. He ate breakfast tacos at a gas station on the outskirts of town, then drove up Old Highway 6 and took the kayak from the back of the truck. From there, he carried the boat over his head across the length of three football fields before he reached the Navasota River. He worked up a sweat while holding the kayak overhead as well as a large packsack that was full of fishing gear, and an insulated lunch box strapped across his back. All those years in the Army kept him in top physical condition, and he continued to lift weights, run and swim after he retired.

Once on the river, he calculated it was about seven miles before he would take the kayak out of the water near the Texas 105 overpass. Along the way, he flicked a 1/32-ounce jig toward the banks of the shallow, slow-moving river, fishing for white bass and crappie. He caught a few fish, including a white bass about a foot long before he grounded the kayak on a sandbar, then ate a sandwich and drank a quart of a berry flavored sports drink for lunch.

His retirement years were dedicated to ventures in real estate, fishing and hunting, and reading. Mostly he read about Texas history, and he was especially intrigued by the battles that had been fought there, clear back to when the Spanish governor, Juan de Ugalde, was entrenched in campaigns against Apaches in northern Coahuila, and in the Texas Hill Country, during the late eighteenth century. Later, the Spanish Royalist Army waged battles against those that wanted to liberate Mexico and Texas from Spain. Eventually the Republic of Mexico and the Texas colonists were at each other's throats in the battles of Velasco, Nacogdoches, Gonzales, San Patricio, Agua Dulce Creek, The Alamo, and others. As Texas wrestled independence from Mexico, it resumed hostilities against various Native Americans tribes in the region during the battles of the Knobs, Stone Houses, Brushy Creek, Neches, Plum Creek, Village Creek, and Bandera Pass. Fighting between Mexico and Texas rekindled in 1842, and the annexation of Texas into the United States in 1845 led to the Mexican War and the siege of Fort Texas near Rancho de Carricitos, the first major battle at Palo Alto, the ensuing fight at Resaca de la Palma, and the U.S. invasion of Mexico.

The men who fought for Texas were ordinary people, with all the flaws of the human condition despite what history books had to say about them. People like Colonel Henry Perry, who led Mexico's Republican Army of the North against the Spaniards at Alazán Creek in 1813, then lost his life in 1817 during the Battle of El Perdido. And the colonist, Randal Jones, who was commissioned by Stephen F. Austin to conduct a raid against the Karankawa tribe at the Battle of Jones Creek in 1824. There was James Bowie's fight at Calf Creek in 1831, and Captain John Austin's victory against a superior Mexican force at the Battle of Velasco in 1832.

Since he was from Georgia, Maurice had an outsider's view of Texas history. He was fascinated by it all. As it is with the story of just about every place, the account of Texas, and how it came to be, was a book of adventure and bloodshed. As he sat on the sandbar eating his lunch, a spotted sandpiper foraged nearby. The bird skittered across the sand, looking for food while keeping an eye on him. How wonderful to be that bird and its uncomplicated life. For people, they want unpleasant things to end and good times to last forever, but unable to do much about it, their lives just bring them to the same place, uninvited residents in a graveyard. They just end up there, almost always well before they planned.

The fish were biting that day. Mostly crappie. The Navasota River did not have a reputation for producing big fish. It was too shallow, for one thing. There were some sizeable gar and freshwater drum in the river, which starts near Mount Calm northeast of Waco and runs 125 miles to the confluence with the Brazos River. Maurice wondered what it would be like to set a hook into a big channel catfish and shoot it in the head, just as he was bringing it up to the kayak, with his Ruger 44. Maybe they'd shoot Robert Pruett in the head like that rather than tie him down for the lethal injection. He wasn't sure why that notion took hold of him, but he brought the pistol with him everywhere as a matter of habit. He could lend it to the executioner and let him plug the convicted murderer right in the head, splattering his brains all over the wall. They might accept it as payment for all the bad that man had done, whether he had done it at all. The evidence against him wasn't much more than people saying he had done it, anyway.

It was at times like that, daydreaming on the river, when he thought about pulling up stakes and running off with Chloe to the Netherlands, or France, perhaps. Leave everything behind. Start a new account somewhere they had never been. His mind wandered like that, without warning, and he would stay with it for hours, working out the details even though he was quite certain nothing would come of it.

He brought the kayak from the water and hid it under a highway overpass, then hitched a ride back to his truck. He had dinner at a restaurant that served smoked barbecue on Highway 6, where he ate a slab of ribs and drank a pitcher of beer. The restaurant was within walking distance of the bed and breakfast, and the walk gave him time to think some more. He had been feeling more tired and lonely than usual of late. Upon returning to his room, he opened a bottle of Scottish whiskey he had been holding onto for years. There was nothing worth watching on television. He pulled a piece of paper from his breast pocket. It was a poem Joe Cuero had written and sent to him a few years back. He kept it with him always because he encouraged Joe to keep writing, and Joe had sent him the original piece of paper, which was written in pen and torn from a composition notebook and was frayed on the left edge. He took a swig of whiskey and read the poem again.

The Funeral

I wonder what the broken,
blood red, dead roses
had been thinking on that cold day in winter.

I wonder how much they suffered
yesterday, and the days that went before it
saying farewell to those who could no longer hear.

I wonder what will happen to them tomorrow
not knowing fear any longer
as we lay them to rest.

Maurice folded the paper and tucked it into his breast pocket. He felt a familiar darkness coming over him. He remembered fondly how, not long before, Fisher told him his wife had come back to him. Fisher had called him to share the good news.

He took another drink of whiskey and smiled at the thought of it. There was never anything worth watching on television, he realized. He took the paper from his pocket again and smoothed it out the best he could on a table. Again, he brought the bottle to his lips and took a few swallows. Putting a dent in that bottle now, for sure, feeling the liquid searing its way down into him and the numbness seeping into his head, he picked up the Ruger, put the barrel in his mouth and pulled the trigger.

22

Fisher got on a plane and went to Texas for the funeral. The plane landed on a Friday night in Austin. Joe was waiting for him. The moon was half full, and they drove along dark streets, past wearied souls drifting around like ghosts. Lights seeped from the windows of buildings. They drove through a park until they crossed the Colorado River, stopped on a narrow street and walked into a dive bar. It was far enough away from the downtown area and its neon lights and counterfeit people, invented personalities and forged smiles. The little bar had a run-down jukebox. Fisher put in a few quarters, banged the machine with his fist to get the coins to drop, and chose a song by Lefty Frizzell.

A small television set was showing the Texas Longhorns' game from the previous weekend. They drank beer and Tennessee whiskey, and shared memories of old Sarge, and Austin Briggs. Joe drank the local beer. Fisher ordered Miller from a tap at the bar. His attitude was contemptuous toward anything that came from Texas, especially when he was drinking. The proprietor of the bar was a Brazilian woman named Polyana. She brought them a tray with fresh mugs of beer and glasses with whiskey and ice.

"What's wrong, Joe?" she asked.

"Our old platoon sergeant died," Joe said.

"Oh, no. I'm so sorry."

"It's alright. This is my friend from the Army. We were in Iraq together. He came down from Philadelphia for the funeral tomorrow."

"Just wait. I'll bring you something special."

Polyana walked away from the table. They sat without saying anything for some time. Fisher had his elbows on the table and glanced upward. Brown streaks smeared the ceiling where water pipes had burst some time ago. The interior of the room was dim and almost empty, except for a few people sitting at the bar. Polyana came back with three glasses filled with an opaque liquid, ice and lime wedges.

"I hope this helps," she said. "I made it with cachaça. Let's get fixed up for your friend, okay? Alright." She held one of the drinks she had made above the table. Fisher and Joe did likewise until all three glasses of the concoction were touching. "All creatures are driven to action by their own nature," Polyana said. "Here's to your friend. It's how we say, pendurar as chuteiras; your friend has hung his boots and we'll see him again someday."

"Salud," Fisher said.

They drank their caipirinhas and placed the glasses on the table.

"You like it?" Polyana asked. "You feel better?"

"Yes."

"Be careful with Joe. He's something when it comes to drinking." She leaned closer to Fisher. "Did Joe tell you about my brother? He's a hit man in Ecuador."

"I'll take another caipirinha," Joe said.

"Me too."

"Can I finish the story? You see, the hit men in Ecuador are known for being terrible shots. Which is ironic, because they have so much work to do," said Polyana, her sultry lips curled in an impish smile as she turned and went to get another round. She had a friendly manner and Fisher admired her as she walked away, a bounce in her gait, like a young girl that had just won a prize, and she was on her way to claim it.

"Hey, snap out of it," Joe said. "Don't go falling in love with the bartender."

"Fuck you," Fisher laughed as he raised a shot of whiskey to his lips. "She's a nice lady, though. Nice body, too. What's with the Ecuadorian hit man shit? I don't get it. Is that a Brazilian joke?"

"She tells that story to all the newcomers."

A short, chiseled Mexican with a stubble of black hair on his head and sideburns approached them and said,"Hey, Joe."

"Hey, Rodrigo. This is my Army buddy, Fisher. Fisher, this is Rodrigo. He was in the Marines. Rodrigo and I met at a gay bar here in Austin."

"Fuck you, Joe," Rodrigo said. "Check it out, man," he said, leaning toward Fisher. "I met this guy at a creative writing class at Texas State. He's a damn good writer, but he's also a smartass."

"Tell me about it," Fisher said.

"Polyana is bringing drinks, why don't you sit down?"

"Naw, man. I'm on my way home. Just wanted to say hey. I'll catch up with you next time, alright?" Rodrigo said.

"You got friends, Manny. That's good."

"Been living here awhile," said Joe.

"You stayed with that Army thing, and they're trying to kick you out on a medical discharge. That's fucked up, Manny. I hope you make it."

"At this point I don't care anymore. You know when you're done, you know? I can say one thing for sure, the Army fucked up my marriage. I don't think me and Viviane are gonna make it. Hell, I can't blame her. I can admit where I fucked up, but at the same time I gotta say, the Army fucked up my marriage."

"Just don't check out like Maurice," Fisher interjected.

"I ain't gonna lie. I've been close a few times over the years. Real close."

"That shit would kill me if you did that, Manny. Not gonna bullshit you. I'm just gonna trust you call me if you ever get close to feeling like that."

"Likewise."

"Oh, no doubt. No fucking doubt. I wouldn't ask you to do anything I wouldn't do, and everybody gets into the dark places sometimes, like Briggs used to say. As long as you know how to get yourself out."

"When we were coming up in the Army, I used to think dudes that asked for help were pussies. I thought of them as weak, but we were trained to think that way," Joe said.

"No doubt, Manny. The shit was real for me, you know? We were dogface soldiers, on the Marne Express to Iraq, back and forth for years. Wasn't no time to be taking a knee, right? That shit was real."

"So, what the fuck you been doing?" asked Joe. "I mean, it's one thing to stay in touch, but now we're sitting here face to face, like we always said we would, but not like this. Our old platoon daddy got us together again. It's something to see you, brother."

"That's real. I ain't doin' a whole lot. Hanging around the house in Philly. Going fishing and hunting, a little this, a little that. I'm good. My daughter is working on her degree to be a teacher. It's a shit job, but I gotta give it to her. She's got a big heart."

"You're blessed. That's incredible. You never brought her down here for her quinceañera though, you asshole."

Fisher burst into laughter at the mention of it. "Shit, I forgot about that. Damn, Manny, what the fuck? I haven't thought about that in a long time."

"Just fucking with you. You can call it good fortune or a blessing. Whatever you wanna call it, you got it. You got everything, and everything that you got, you deserve it."

"Why are you talking like that, Manny? You alright?"

"No bullshit?"

"No bullshit. What's up?"

Joe looked around the room. There was not a person within ten feet of them in the bar. "I'm not sure, but I might be going a little crazy. This is what I'm talking about. There came a point when I decided it was time to take a knee. What difference was it gonna make at that point? My marriage was on the rocks, I couldn't sleep, I was flying off the handle, all that shit. I got to thinking, what does it matter what anybody thinks to begin with? The Army, my peers, my soldiers, whatever. I paid my dues, and they couldn't touch me. They didn't do what I did, they didn't see what I saw, so fuck it. When it was all said and done, I needed to get some help, so that's what I did. I asked for help, and I got help. But I also saw for myself that the stigma is still there. It's real, brother. The fucked-up thing about it is that they throw you aside in such a subtle way, you might not even notice. But I said fuck it, I'm all in on this one. There's no turning back once you start down that road. These days, it's like I can't even breathe unless I'm alone."

Joe hesitated while Polyana brought them another round, they all had another drink in memory of Maurice, and she went away.

"Don't stop, Manny. Keep going."

"Alright. It was Briggs. I used to talk to him in my dreams. He would be there, in Iraq. We would all be there. And I honestly don't know what it was. For me, it wasn't just bad luck or whatever you want to call it. When Briggs checked out on his first day back in Iraq, something happened to me. They sent me to Germany, and I was looking at these birds outside my window at the hospital. And I was wishing, it's crazy, but I was wishing his spirit was in one of those birds when it was looking right at me. Then I started having nightmares."

Joe closed his eyes. "I ain't gonna do this. I told myself I wasn't, anyway."

"Are you religious?"

"You know what I am. What difference does it make?"

Fisher pulled a coin from his pocket and put it on the table. "Render to Caesar the things that are Caesar's, and to God the things that belong to God."

Then Fisher reached over and patted Joe on the arm. "Take another shot," he told Joe. Fisher stood up. "I gotta hit the latrine," he said.

"Alright."

Joe opened his eyes and watched Fisher depart. He picked up the glass and took another shot of whiskey, turned the glass upside down, and placed it back on the table. He waved at Polyana and motioned for another round and saw Fisher coming back. Joe could see Fisher had been taking care of himself over the years. He looked lean and fit, just as he did when he was in the Army.

"Say," said Fisher. "We got more drinks coming?"

"They're on the way."

"You know what I was thinking?"

"No, but you're probably gonna tell me."

"Is it true what they say about Austin? Do they have any weed around here?"

"Nobody in here's holding as far as I know. But I got my private stash right here in my pocket. I got a buddy that does the drug tests for my unit, so I'm covered and I'm always holding."

"When we gonna fire one up?"

"Oh, I'd say right after the next round."

"Where we gonna do that?"

"In my truck, I suppose. That old piece of shit parked out front is all I got left."

"I'm gonna get high in Texas."

"We'd probably end up in Mexico if it weren't for the funeral tomorrow."

"Going down there ain't on my bucket list, Manny."

"Well, me either. But sometimes it just works out that way."

Fisher frowned and took another shot. "Thanks for letting me know."

They went outside and Joe rolled a joint as they sat in his truck, parked across the street from the bar. The sidewalks were empty. Somewhere in the distance, people were listening to live music, closer to downtown. "This used to be a black neighborhood before they started building condos and townhomes near the interstate. It hasn't made it this far, yet." Joe smiled at Fisher while explaining the gentrification of East Austin.

"Shitheads."

"That's progress," Joe said. "These assholes came in here years ago with big tech, computers and shit, and it ruined this town. It absolutely ruined it."

"Aren't they gonna leave anything for the blacks and the Mexicans?"

"I wouldn't bet on it," said Joe, lighting up. "This is what they call the elite class, moving in and taking over. Kind of like what we did in Iraq."

"Jesus Christ, you barely started smoking and you're gonna get all philosophical on me now?"

"Fuck it all," Joe said, and passed the spliff to Fisher. "Don't think of it like that if you don't want to, but they're getting rid of this neighborhood. The blacks and browns are moving out, and the rent keeps getting higher. Besides, who wants to live here now? There's a bunch of dudes with Birkenstocks walking around here during the day. The neighborhood smells like pachouli and gourmet coffee, and people are driving Audis and riding around on electric scooters. It's fucking embarrassing what they're doing to this place."

"Damn, Manny. That's depressing."

"That's what's going down, brother."

Fisher took a hit and passed it back to Joe. They were both drunk, and the marijuana was starting to kick in.

"You're a fucking trip, Manny."

"I've paid my dues. They couldn't kill me in Iraq and they're not gonna run me out of this town. I'll mop the floor with one of these fucking yuppies someday."

"That ain't saying much, but I don't think yuppies have been around since the eighties. Is that what they call them around here?"

Joe turned and looked at Fisher, pondering the question.

"Oh, I don't know. I think they're all shitheads. Let's forget about them and go back to my place, drink some more, and smoke."

23

The funeral for Maurice Young came and went, as did the rest of autumn. Winter came, and Joe sat in his kitchen, smoking a joint and reading Tim O'Brien's novel, *The Things They Carried*. His wife had moved out. She had gone back and forth, in and out of his life, numerous times. This time, she took all her clothes with her one day as she left the house to go to work.

Voices screamed inside his head as she sat next to him, paying bills on his desktop computer. If he tried to find a positive in the situation, he was sure he would only be lying to himself. He was going through the motions, sure that she was never coming back even though she told him she had not made a final decision.

Joe did not trust anyone. He read somewhere that PTSD made people withdraw from others. It was the nature of the injury to do so. His wife walked away from him after walking by his side for ten years, trying to get him to seek help. Once he did, she decided she had to leave. He did not want to lash out at her because he was sure that it was all his fault.

One night he went for a walk, trying to find peace of mind. He could not focus on anything except the cold air. Neighbors had decorated their homes with Christmas lights, which made him feel empty inside. He went home and fell asleep, then woke up at two-thirty in the morning.

Like a ray of sunshine, his wife texted him. She wanted to go holiday shopping and have lunch that afternoon. He was happy for the first time in ages. Later in the day when their date was over, he felt the same emptiness and frustration. He went for a walk around the neighborhood to clear his head, but it did not work. He took his second shower of the day, not because he needed to, but there was nothing else to do. He wrote in his journal. He ate food.

His wife told him a long time ago that when they first got together, she thought about him all the time. Now she was out on her own, trying to see if she got to feeling that way again. He could not think of anything she could say that could be like that, and all the emotions it brought to the surface. He wanted to remember that feeling when he got to the bad places in his head. Lately he had been in the dark all the time and he hated it. He wanted to stay out of his irrationality. He would be so much better off, but it was so familiar to him that he would end up there without knowing how, like being on a long trip and realizing he was home already.

Time passed without motivation to try anything new. He had been feeling peaceful and calm, cautiously moving forward. He and his wife had been spending more time together, getting to know each other again. The holidays were difficult. He went home on a Friday afternoon, took a painkiller at four-thirty and awoke in a haze seven hours later. The depression returned and he took another pill, but not because he was in physical pain. He drifted back to sleep thinking of a conversation he had with his wife about her search for a new place to live, as if to say she was never coming back. He had tried to be supportive while not showing it was tearing him up inside.

He could have been fortune telling all those months and not have predicted his wife would return in the middle of the night. A feeling of awkwardness came over him as they laid down together and she fell asleep. He remembered something the crime novelist, Raymond Chandler, said: A good story cannot be devised; it has to be distilled.

Joe realized life was the same way. It was the end of another year, when folks started planning a new direction for their lives. He knew it would be foolish for him to do so, for it would explode on takeoff like a rocket at Cape Canaveral. The days of the calendar had no meaning anymore.

24

It was nighttime, and a half-moon provided light as Fisher walked among the trees of an apple orchard. Memories of hunting with his father guided him in the Pennsylvania woods. Freezing temperatures and heavy snow covered the mountain. It was the day after Christmas, and he carried a flintlock rifle with him. After crossing the orchard, he found the trail that cut through a stand of hemlock trees. It was dark inside the densely populated hemlock stand, even during daytime. If a wounded animal went in there, a hunter would have difficulty finding it and backbreaking work dragging it out.

When Fisher was a boy, the woods frightened him. He would imagine a bear lunging out of the thick stand of trees. Legend had it there were Indian burial grounds in there, or someplace else on the mountain. There was a cabin on the edge of the orchard. Stories of hauntings and past hunts from years gone by would be told around the warmth of a cast iron stove. Those were the days when he was a boy. Now he was a man. Maybe he was a fool to think of such things, but they kept him company as he made his way to the top of the ridge. His feet were numb, and his heart thumped in his chest as he reached his destination, having trudged through fresh snow for half an hour to get there.

The ridgeline overlooked a sparsely wooded hollow, and at the bottom of the hollow was a creek. He sat on a log and leaned back against a fir tree, its branches laden with heavy snow. Morning's grey haze was still more than an hour away. As he wiped the sweat from his brow with a bandana, the quiet of the forest was interrupted by the soft exhale of his breath, and the occasional drip of water from the fir tree.

A thermos of hot coffee was in his pack, but he was content to listen to the grand silence of the woods. Out in the darkness, there were deer foraging among fields that had been harvested long ago. As dawn approached, they would head for safety in the deep woods. He chose the ridgeline as a likely place where the deer would cross between feeding and seeking cover.

He was likely the only person on the mountain that day. A blizzard had swept in. He spent Christmas day in a hotel nearby, eating meatloaf sandwiches his wife made for him. Ever since the funeral, she knew he was headed back to the woods upstate to get away that winter. There would be other holidays together, with love and harmony. But not this season. Leaning against the tree, he listened half-heartedly for signs of life. As always, he did not care whether he shot a deer or not. If he did, he would have to gut the animal and carry it in his truck, all the way to a butcher in the city.

A new day approached. A snowy spell of dreamland and nothing, leftover thoughts from walking. Staring into the dark, barren winter, wondering what was coming next. He believed in nothing for the first time he could remember. He brought from his youth memories of a frightened boy in a world of violence, the only bond that seemed to bring people together. His only escape was the woods of northern Pennsylvania, the only place he could breathe. Every place else was a fight.

He sat there against the tree for a long time and thought of his daughter, out there somewhere far away. Settled down with a family of her own. Not asking him for anything. He nodded off in the bitter cold. His rifle sat next to him. Like him, it was good in heavy cover. Useful for cutting through the muck, but not much of anything else. He thought about the bullies he fought on the schoolyards and how Maurice taught him a Buddhism verse about Secret Refuge:

From within a state of free from grasping and beyond intellect,
I take refuge in the nature of the great expanse
of sameness and perfection,
Atemporal emptiness, free from conceptual elaboration,
Primordially pure in essence, natural expression
and compassionate energy.

He was at one time in his life a killer, a destroyer in the ways the Army taught him. He did not feel anything back then, stuffed deep into a compartment. A weapon designed for a singular purpose. Looking down at his enemy, their flesh torn apart by bullets or explosives, was something he never forgot. Human eyes glazed over in death's shock, and with no light in them. The eyes of the dead were always like that.

Dawn approached as he stirred from sleep. A fresh set of bear tracks led from the top of the ridge down toward the creek. He was tired. His spirit was a hunter taking in the comfort of an iron stove burning hickory logs, filling the cabin with warmth as other hunters told stories of their adventures in the woods. Glimpses of an elusive bobcat. A snowshoe hare picking its way on the edge of a forest. A barred owl swooping out of a tree at dusk. The blur of a grouse as it exploded from cover, taking flight.

Few had seen a night giving way to dawn such as this. Echoes from the creek bed. Archaic were the sounds of nature as the woods came to life. Rock ledges and trees took shape. Fresh snow hastened the presence of dim light. Suddenly there was movement. The silhouette of a fox as it hunted, leaping high and diving, probing the snow with its snout. He watched as the fox faded away among the trees below. An owl hooted nearby, but he could not see it.

The moon went away. Something else stirred below, unseen. Something small, and he could not make it out. He waited, but it brought nothing. The woods were quiet again.

It occurred to him to get up and leave the forest to its magic. He was an intruder, an unwelcome collector. Or at least pick another location. This place was too perfect in its natural sorcery and he didn't belong there. Life was everywhere, albeit silent. He tried not to think. The way of dawn was coming, and any movement by him would spoil it. The surrounding woods were a steep hill covered in snow.

Nothing could stop the sun. It crept over the horizon. Water dripped from the limbs of naked trees, pattering against the ground. In the first sliver of daylight, Fisher saw crystals of snow dazzling on the ground. It was wonderful and strange, as if he had never seen it before. He sat there and shivered.

There were reasons for going upstate, into the mountains during winter. A burst of air swept in and rushed through the trees, causing them to sway and creak. He fixed his gaze toward the bottom of the ridge. There had to be something down there. He sat still, shivering against the cold as he peered into the forest below.

The mountain paid no attention to him. It was not logical for him to be there. But logic had very little to do with anything. Even if a deer were to pass by, he would not bother with the rifle. He was not there to take a life. There was no reason to kill that day. He had come to the mountain for the search, to turn himself inside out, and to find his other self, the secret enemy that dwelled inside him. If he kept looking, he might find it somewhere in the expanse of the mountain and get hold of it. Then he would take his knife and slaughter it, blood pouring like wax onto the snow to fatten the land.

End

www.ingramcontent.com/pod-product-compliance
Lightning Source LLC
LaVergne TN
LVHW031337150826
845673LV00012B/2941

* 9 7 8 1 6 5 7 2 9 5 6 7 4 *